"We need to talk..."

Tisha didn't particularly like Russell's tone. What was going on with him? Did he have a change of heart about them before she got the chance to disclose the secrets she kept? Or did he have secrets of his own to reveal?

"Come in," she told him. "What do you want to talk about?"

"Leah Redfield," Russell said tonelessly.

What did he know about Leah? Had she confided in him about her situation? "What about Leah?" she asked tentatively.

He folded his arms. "She was found dead in her car." He spoke sharply.

"What?" Her voice shook. "How?"

"An apparent single self-inflicted gunshot wound to the head."

"Oh, no." She put a hand to her mouth, disbelieving that Leah would have killed herself. Could she have?

Russell peered at her. "Before I jump to any wrong conclusions, is there something you want to tell me...?"

"Yes, a few things." Her shoulders slumped.

Under the circumstances, she didn't see how she could possibly remain silent about who she was... especially with him.

"Leah is my handler with the US Marshals Service. I'm in the federal Witness Security Program."

In memory of my beloved mother, Marjah Aljean, a devoted lifetime fan of Harlequin romances, who inspired me to do my very best in finding success in my personal and professional lives. To H. Loraine, the true love of my life, whose support has been unwavering through the many years together; and to the loyal fans of my romance, mystery, suspense and thriller fiction published over the years. Lastly, a nod goes out to my wonderful editors, Allison Lyons and Denise Zaza, for the opportunity to lend my literary voice and creative spirit to the Harlequin Intrigue line.

SPECIAL AGENT WITNESS

R. BARRI FLOWERS

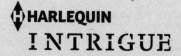

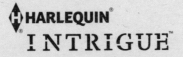

Recycling programs for this product may not exist in your area.

ISBN-13: 978-1-335-59118-0

Special Agent Witness

Copyright © 2023 by R. Barri Flowers

For questions and comments about the quality of this book, please contact us at CustomerService@Harlequin.com.

Harlequin Enterprises ULC
22 Adelaide St. West, 41st Floor
Toronto, Ontario M5H 4E3, Canada
www.Harlequin.com

Printed in U.S.A.

R. Barri Flowers is an award-winning author of crime, thriller, mystery and romance fiction featuring three-dimensional protagonists, riveting plots, unexpected twists and turns, and heart-pounding climaxes. With an expertise in true crime, serial killers and characterizing dangerous offenders, he is perfectly suited for the Harlequin Intrigue line. Chemistry and conflict between the hero and heroine, attention to detail and incorporating the very latest advances in criminal investigations are the cornerstones of his romantic suspense fiction. Discover more on popular social networks and Wikipedia.

Visit the Author Profile page at Harlequin.com.

CAST OF CHARACTERS

Rosamund Santiago/Tisha González—A Homeland Security Investigations special agent who enters the federal Witness Security Program while awaiting testimony against the human trafficker who murdered her partner. Can she maintain her secret identity from a handsome, curious detective with a hitman in pursuit?

Russell Lynley—A detective for the Weconta Falls Police Department in Northern California who has his eye on the attractive new waitress in town. The former FBI agent soon learns that she is in grave danger and vows to protect her at all costs.

Leah Redfield—The deputy US marshal is the handler for the witness in protection. But can she keep her safe?

Simon Griswold—Ringleader of a human trafficking organization who will stop at nothing to beat the rap against him, including murder.

Harold Paxton—The Dallas Field Office special agent in charge, who needs Rosamund's testimony to make the case against the suspect, with no room for failure.

The Hitman—Hired to kill Rosamund, he is relentless and always accomplishes his mission. Will he be successful again?

Prologue

Homeland Security Investigations Special Agent Rosamund Santiago was on an undercover assignment with her HSI partner, Special Agent Johnnie Langford, in Dallas, Texas. They were on their way to an important make-or-break meeting this evening. *We can't afford any slipups*, she thought, as they headed south. If things went as planned, after a six-month investigation, they would soon put a major human trafficking, sex trafficking, and money laundering operation out of commission. In this undertaking, they were working in conjunction with the U.S. Immigration and Customs Enforcement, Federal Bureau of Investigation, North Texas Trafficking Task Force, and the Dallas Police Department. The primary target and ringleader of the criminal enterprise was a man named Simon Griswold, who pretended to be a reputable businessman, importing antique and contemporary furniture from Mexico and South America. In fact, this was nothing more than a facade for his real mission, which was the human trafficking and sexual exploitation of noncitizens and vulnerable American women and minors, enriching himself and his operatives in the process.

For Rosamund, as important as taking down human traffickers and other criminals was for her career, it was also personal. As a thirty-two-year-old Latina, born and raised in El Paso, Texas, she had witnessed firsthand as a girl the smuggling of humans against their will across the Rio Grande and U.S.–Mexico border, and the even greater cruelties that often awaited them in the states they were dispersed to. She knew then that she wanted to do something to stop this when she was old enough and the opportunity presented itself. It did, once she had completed her Master of Arts degree in Criminology and Criminal Justice from the University of Texas at Arlington and went to work for the Department of Homeland Security's Center for Countering Human Trafficking seven years ago. With literally tens of thousands of human trafficking cases documented in Texas every year, ranging from child trafficking and domestic servitude, to forced prostitution and sexual exploitation, to human smuggling and labor trafficking, Rosamund admittedly had her hands full.

With such a workload, it didn't give her time for a meaningful social life, much less the opportunity to have a serious romance. But this didn't mean she did not long for both at some point. Who wouldn't? As for a love life, she had to believe that if the right person came along, she would know it, and everything else would fall into place. Wouldn't it?

"How you doing over there?" Langford asked as he drove them to the destination in the black Ford Explorer. Part of their work together was their undercover life, posing as an unmarried couple who had gotten comfortable building a lucrative business as human traffickers. In truth, thirty-five-year-old Langford, a ten-year veteran with the Department of Homeland Security, was happily married to a lovely woman named Katie and was the father of two cute and energetic little boys. And the only real involvement between her and Langford was their shared desire to make the world a better place in the small way they could contribute to that happening.

Rosamund realized she had been silent in her reverie. Or feeling slightly tense, as always, whenever an operation was about to go down. She eyed him from the passenger seat. African American, he was as fit as she was, four inches taller at six feet, and had short black hair styled in waves and a line-up cut. His brown eyes were deeper than her own, which were a softer hazel. She forced a smile and said convincingly, "I'm good. Just want this to go without a hitch." She knew they would be meeting Simon Griswold alone, hoping to catch him in a moment of weakness and get just enough additional evidence to what they had already accumulated to make an arrest. At which time, they would really lay the hammer to him in the hopes of breaking up the entire human trafficking ring.

"It will," Langford assured her. "Griswold has no reason to believe this is anything other than business as usual. Whatever he gives us to hang himself, we'll take. And if he has brought any trafficked victims along for the ride, we'll make sure they're taken care of without blowing our cover."

"Okay." She smiled again, realizing this sense of dread she was feeling was nothing more than wanting to get this over with, as always. Griswold was supposed to give them the time and place for the arrival of a tractor trailer that was being used to smuggle noncitizens into the country. Rosamund and Langford would pretend to aid in getting them fake identifications and otherwise helping with integrating them into society and introducing them to would-be exploiters of the trafficked victims. In reality, these were fellow HSI and ICE agents removing them from harm's way.

But should there be any hiccups, there were other investigators on standby, ready and able to come to their assistance, when and if they gave the signal. Beyond that, Rosamund knew she and Langford were armed with Sig Sauer P320-XTEN 10-millimeter striker-fired pistols and wearing ballistic vests. Then there was the fact that she had recently taken up Thai boxing as a means for self-defense and as a combat sport. So, really, what was there to worry about?

They arrived at the Bricks Motel on Appolane Road and parked in the lot. Langford said with a quiet sigh, "Let's get this over with."

"I'm ready," she said calmly and flipped her curly black ponytail for effect. They exited the vehicle and approached Room 110. As they did so, Rosamund got an uneasy feeling. *Something's not quite right*, she thought. The parking lot was lowly lit and there were a few other cars in the lot. She did note the familiar metallic gray BMW iX parked in front of the room. Once they neared it, the driver's-side door opened and the man they were meeting stepped out.

Simon Griswold was forty years old and just under six feet tall with a medium build. He was wearing a dark suit with dark shoes. His salt-and-pepper hair was styled in a pompadour fade. "You're late," he said brusquely.

"Traffic," Langford told him tonelessly.

"In fact, we're actually ten minutes early," Rosamund said, suspecting Griswold was simply pushing their buttons for whatever reason.

"Why don't we go inside?" he said tersely, his blue eyes landing on her briefly.

As they followed him to the door, she again had the sense that something wasn't right. She wondered if they should abort the meeting. But before she could act on this and alert Langford, the door was opened and Langford went inside, along with Griswold. The moment she stepped through the door and Griswold shut it behind her, Rosamund saw he was holding a gun. It looked like a .357 Magnum revolver. The weapon was pointed at Langford, who said angrily, "What is this?"

"You tell me," Griswold responded gruffly. "I don't like doing business with feds."

Langford looked uncomfortable. "I don't know where you got your intel, but it's wrong."

"I don't think so," the human trafficker spat. Before Langford could go for his weapon, Griswold shot him point-blank in the head. She watched with horror as her partner fell to the floor, feeling both helpless and shaken to the core in that moment.

Then out of the corner of her eye, Rosamund spotted movement. A tall and stocky bald-headed man had come out of the bathroom. She turned to see him reach for something inside his leather jacket. A gun. *He plans to kill me too, unless I can beat him to the draw,* she told herself. Instinctively, she pulled out her own weapon and immediately fired at the man, twice, putting him down. She turned back to Griswold to see he had lined her up in his sights for the kill before she could aim her gun at him.

"Goodbye, Special Agent Santiago," he said with a sneer.

As her life flashed before her eyes, Rosamund couldn't see any way out of this. No future to look forward to. No romance with a loving man waiting in the wings. But as she stood there, expecting to be shot in the head like Langford, she saw that Griswold's gun had apparently jammed. As Griswold muttered an expletive, Rosamund realized she now had the upper hand. But before she could use it, Griswold charged her, dislodging the gun from her hand as the two went down.

"I'll kill you with my bare hands," he said.

But as he tried to wrap his thick hands around her neck, Rosamund felt just as confident in her ability to take him in hand-to-hand combat. *I have to fight back or die trying*, she told herself. Relying on quick movements she had learned in her Thai boxing classes, Rosamund slammed both fists into Griswold's temples as hard as she could and then smashed a fist solidly into the top of his bulbous nose, breaking it and rendering him unconscious as he slumped beside her on the hard tile floor.

After quickly handcuffing the man, Rosamund scurried over to her seriously wounded partner and gasped. It didn't take much to realize that Johnnie Langford was gone.

THREE DAYS LATER, Rosamund attended the funeral of Homeland Security Investigations Special Agent Langford, who was laid to rest in a cemetery in his hometown of Beaumont, Texas. His beautiful widow, Katie Langford, was overcome with emotion as the pastor paid tribute to the slain investigator at the graveside service. Standing on opposite sides of her were Katie's sons, Johnnie Jr. and Desmond, ages seven and five, respectively. Both reminded Rosamund of her fallen partner. She couldn't imagine what they must be going through, having lost their dad before ever having enough time to truly get to know him as a father, man, and someone who gave his life fighting crime and victimization.

Rosamund felt both grateful and uneasy that his killer had failed to take her out. Instead, she had turned the tables on him and stopped him from his lethal mission. But even with that victory, she realized there was still much work to be done to destroy the human trafficking operation that had resulted in so much suffering and exploitation. Until she was able to finish the job by testifying against the trafficker, Rosamund knew that Johnnie Langford would never be able to rest in peace.

Chapter One

Rosamund sat on a plush armchair in the large office of the HSI Dallas Field Office special agent in charge Harold Paxton, the fortysomething former Bureau of Alcohol, Tobacco, Firearms and Explosives deputy special agent in charge of the field office in Albuquerque, New Mexico. She informed Paxton that she believed there was a mole in the organization who had caused the death of her partner, Johnnie Langford, at the hands of reputed human trafficker Simon Griswold.

She knew Griswold was now in federal custody and faced a slew of charges, including murder and attempted murder, human smuggling, and the sexual exploitation of women and children. She also knew someone had tipped off Griswold that they were undercover agents, which had cost Langford his life. Rosamund felt it was only by sheer luck, or something akin to a gun malfunctioning miracle, that she had survived Griswold's attempt to silence her for good. It had failed, but she was still reeling from the way things had gone down. Rosamund glanced at her new partner, Virginia Flannery, who was sitting beside her. Virginia was the same age as Rosamund, tall, slender, and attractive, with aquamarine eyes and light blonde hair styled in a feathered pixie. Rosamund imagined she could have chosen any occupation and been successful, with a degree in computing and linguistics from Yale University. Instead, she preferred a career in law enforcement and had been with the DHS for nearly a decade. Though saddened at having lost her partner, Rosamund felt fortunate that his replacement was someone she believed Johnnie would have approved of.

She turned to Harold Paxton, who stood behind his desk wearing a gray suit on a husky frame. He had short red hair and a horseshoe-shaped hairline. Gold-flecked green eyes with bags beneath looked back at her pensively. Next to him was Monroe Cortez, U.S. Marshal for the Northern District of Texas. In his early fifties, he was tall and lean, with short gray hair tapered on the sides and brown eyes behind oval glasses.

"You were right, Agent Santiago," Paxton said with a sigh. "We do seem to have a problem in our midst that needs to be dealt with."

That's an understatement, Rosamund mused. She batted her curly lashes. "With all due respect, Sir, that 'problem' has compromised our entire investigation and got Johnnie Langford killed. It needs more than merely being dealt with." Immediately, Rosamund wished she could take it back, fearing she had overstepped her bounds. She glanced at Virginia, who offered a tiny supportive smile.

"I couldn't agree more," he said levelly. "Losing Langford has affected all of us, up and down the chain. Whoever ratted him out will be discovered and prosecuted to the full extent of the law." Paxton's brow furrowed. "The work you two put in cannot be overstated in nailing those involved in the sordid business of human trafficking. And cannot be further jeopardized by having someone come after you too. Your testimony key in successfully prosecuting Simon Griswold. It will have a ripple effect on his entire operation."

"I'm aware of that," she told him, feeling the pressure of needing to stay alive. "And I will certainly take any necessary steps to ensure my safety."

"Unfortunately, we'll need to go further than that," he said. "Since Griswold is desperate to keep you from testifying, making you a sitting duck is simply not an option."

Rosamund swallowed. "So, what are you saying? Round-the-clock protection?" She tried to imagine having to wine and dine security at her place while essentially giving up her privacy. But wasn't that preferable to being killed?

"We'll be placing you in the federal witness security program," Paxton stated with a straight face.

"What?" For a moment, Rosamund thought she misunderstood him.

Then he reiterated it. "We need to keep you out of harm's way till Griswold goes to trial in a few months. I know this may seem extreme, but—"

She interrupted him, "Witness security program, really?" The thought of what that could entail unnerved Rosamund. "Can't you assign marshals or even a secret service detail to protect me?" She glanced at Monroe Cortez, who remained impassive.

"We intend to do the former. Not so much the latter." Paxton rubbed his jutting chin for a beat. "In this instance, even that is insufficient for protecting you."

Rosamund sensed there was more to this. "What aren't you telling me?" *Or will I need to figure it out myself?* she thought uneasily.

He paused again, his forehead wrinkled. "We have good reason to believe that Simon Griswold put a hit out on you."

"What?" she said, chilled at the notion.

"According to one of our informants, Griswold has hired an unidentified professional assassin to take you out," Paxton told her bluntly. "Griswold figures that with you out of the way, he walks. He has a good point. Your testimony and corroborating evidence are enough to put him away for life. But if you die, with Langford no longer around to testify in court, the case against Griswold could very well fall apart. It's a chance we're not willing to take." He flashed his eyes at Cortez. "This is where the U.S. Marshals Service comes in. Till we go to trial, under the WITSEC, they'll be relocating you, and providing a new identity and authentic credentials to that effect. U.S. Marshal Cortez will coordinate this and brief you accordingly."

"I'll be happy to answer any questions you have, Agent Santiago," Cortez spoke up.

Indeed, Rosamund did have more questions than she could get out at once, unsure precisely how this would work. But one question in particular came to mind. "When exactly will this go into effect?"

"It already has," Cortez responded matter-of-factly. "From this point on, your life is no longer your own, per se." Cortez looked at Paxton for help.

"You won't be able to go back to your apartment," Paxton advised her. "It's too dangerous. Agent Flannery will drop by, accompanied by deputy marshals, to collect a few personal items and clothing and that's it. You'll need to hand over your cell phone and laptop, along with any other devices that have information that can identify or track you and possibly lead a hired killer to your whereabouts."

Virginia touched her shoulder. "I'll be sure to keep my intrusion into your personal space as minimal as possible," she uttered sympathetically. "And it will be just as you left it upon your return."

"Thank you," Rosamund acknowledged, knowing she was only doing her job.

"Sorry our newfound partnership will be short-lived," Virginia said. "But we can pick up where we left off once the threat has been neutralized and Simon Griswold and his cronies have been put away in federal prison for the rest of their lives."

Rosamund nodded. *Griswold deserves nothing less after his coldblooded murder of Johnnie*, she thought. Same for his partners in the crimes involved within human trafficking. She looked forward to coming out of this on the other end and resuming her career as an HSI special agent. That was, assuming she was successful in hiding from Griswold's hired assassin. The fact that he was willing to take this to such extremes made it clear that he feared what she knew and would say in court to take him down. She had to abide by the rules if she was to successfully testify against Griswold and reclaim her life.

As if to hammer down those sentiments and sense of urgency, Paxton, with his thick brows knitted, said, "I don't think I need to tell you, Agent Santiago, just how important it is for you and the DHS's Center for Countering Human Trafficking, along with the other agencies involved, to keep you alive and able to do your job as laid out."

"I'm able and willing to do what's necessary, Sir," Rosamund made clear, in spite of some concerns about making the needed adjustments that came with a new life. How could she not acquiesce, consider-

ing the alternative? "You can count on me to coop-
erate fully."

For the first time since she'd come into his office,
Harold Paxton flashed a smile. "I was hoping you'd
say that." He glanced at Cortez. "Well, let's get this
over with, and in no time flat Simon Griswold will
pay the price for all his illegal activities and then we
can all go about our business of enforcing the law
against other lowlifes like him."

Rosamund grinned in an act of cooperation, even
while feeling butterflies in her stomach in taking on
a new and unexpected challenge in her career.

ROSAMUND HAD BEEN temporarily relocated to Weconta Falls, a small, picturesque waterfront town
tucked away in Northern California, not too far from
the San Francisco Bay Area. Admittedly, this was the
type of place Rosamund could have imagined retir-
ing to, with its peaceful environment, abundance of
Douglas fir, Western hemlock, and tanoak evergreen
trees, and parks, and running trails. Problem was
that her desired retirement was years, if not decades,
away. Rosamund would have preferred to be back
on the job, trying to do her part to put away the bad
guys. Such as Simon Griswold. But she needed to lay
low until such time when her testimony could wipe
the smugness off his face, even as he awaited trial.

In the interim, she was now Tisha González. Rosamund had chosen the name as a combination of her

beloved late grandmother's middle name and the last name of a childhood friend, Maria, before she married and took her husband's surname. Rosamund felt the new name had a nice ring to it, even if she lived for the day when she no longer needed to use it. But for the time being, she would do whatever was asked of her if it meant staying alive.

That included not drawing undue attention to herself, while still trying to fit into her new surroundings. Presently, she was at the Creek Crust Townhouses complex on Fenella Street, where she had been provided an end unit on a dead-end street.

"Well, here it is," voiced her handler, Leah Redfield. The deputy U.S. marshal was in her midthirties and well-proportioned on a five-foot-nine frame. She had short red hair in a pixie bob cut and blue eyes. This was her fifth year on the job and second as a divorcée. "Probably not what you were used to, huh?"

Rosamund sized up the downstairs. Fully furnished with contemporary furniture, it was pleasant enough with a separate living room, dining room, den, and kitchen, with engineered hardwood flooring and faux wood blinds on bay windows. *I'll make it livable*, she told herself. But still, she already missed her spacious split-level loft, with its floor-to-ceiling fiberglass windows, vinyl plank floors, and bamboo furniture. "It's fine," she told the handler, committed to trying to make the most of it.

"Why don't we take a look upstairs," Leah said.

Rosamund followed her up the staircase and found two bedrooms similar in size and with furnishings matching those downstairs. Again, not her taste, but it would have to do for as long as she was a resident of Weconta Falls. And who knew how long that would last. They went back to the main floor and Rosamund noted the door off the kitchen. She asked, "Where does that lead to?"

"Actually, I was just about to show you." Leah opened the door. "It's a direct access to the garage. And your car."

"Really?" Rosamund stepped into the garage, curious. In her other life, she had recently purchased a Subaru Forester Sport. She eyed the silver vehicle.

"It's a Hyundai Elantra," Leah told her. "Comes with GPS to help you get around more easily. Keys are inside."

"Hmm…okay." Rosamund was ready to take it for a test drive, but that would have to come later, as they went back inside the townhouse.

"There's a security system," Leah said. "It's a pretty safe area, so there shouldn't be any problems, generally speaking."

"Good." Rosamund nodded, while thinking that an assassin was past the point of generally speaking, should he or she ever find her location before the trial. So a security system was an important part of her safety. Along with her firearm, one of the few things she had been allowed to keep in her new life as a means for self-defense.

"Using the program's vast resources and connections with a temp agency, we were able to find you a job as a waitress at a restaurant in town," Leah was saying. "I looked at your file and saw that you did some waitressing in college. So this should be a piece of cake for you and save the trouble of looking for something yourself."

Rosamund frowned. "I'm still drawing my salary, but not able to access it, of course," she pointed out, which was the least her employers could have done for an involuntary reassignment until it was over. In the meantime, before this went into effect, she was able to draw out some cash from her savings that had been tucked away for a rainy day, which this certainly qualified as.

"That's great you're still getting paid. Not all persons under witness protection are afforded that luxury." Leah smoothed a thin brow. "But it's important for you to give the guise, if nothing else, of fitting in with a normal life so as not to stand out. Working in a job that doesn't draw much attention is part of that process."

"I understand," Rosamund relented. "Don't mean to be difficult." Or maybe venting a little made her feel better about the situation. She forced a grin. "When do I start?" She hoped the waitressing all came back to her in a snap.

"Tomorrow," her handler said. "All you need to do is show up. The sooner you get acclimated, the better."

Rosamund nodded. "Juggling dishes and drinks, here I come," she joked.

Leah chuckled. "Well, I'll let you get settled in."

"All right." She walked her to the door, while Rosamund wondered what the future had in store for her as she navigated this new life under an assumed name.

"Oh, I almost forgot." Leah turned around and pulled out a cell phone from her leather jacket. "This is for you." She handed it to Rosamund. "It's a secure line and you'll always be able to reach me whenever you need to. I'm sure it goes without saying that you're not to use it to contact family, friends, colleagues, you get the picture. Anyone from your former life who has even an inkling of your whereabouts could put you in danger, along with themselves."

"Got it." Rosamund clutched the cell phone to her chest. One of the most painful things in leaving Dallas was not even being able to call her parents and younger sister to say goodbye. But those were the rules of WITSEC, along with temporarily removing access to credit cards, bank accounts, social networks, and any other traceable means for someone out to kill her. She was more than up to the task, having no desire to jeopardize the safety of anyone she cared about.

Leah smiled. "Then I'll be on my way." She gave her a supportive look. "Good luck with this."

Rosamund smiled back. "Thanks." She saw her out and peeked through the window as Leah got into her official vehicle, a red Buick Encore, and drove off. Alone for the first time since all this started, Rosamund got the measure of the place she would be calling home for the foreseeable future. She ended up in the en suite of the primary bedroom. Glancing at her reflection in the mirror above a soapstone countertop, she took note of the new hairstyle. Her previously mid-back-length curly dark hair, cut in a U-shaped blunt style, was now medium length in a layered lob. She liked it, but it would still take some getting used to. It hadn't been a prerequisite of the program, but more of a precautionary move to make her appearance that much different than before. What hadn't changed was having a complexion that made it unnecessary to wear much, if any, makeup. *Hopefully, I'll fit right in with the surroundings and new job*, she told herself. As though she had much of a choice. Not when it came down to that in order to stay alive.

THE HITMAN WONDERED where the pretty Homeland Security Investigations special agent was hiding. Rosamund Santiago had seemingly vanished into thin air. At least that was what Special Agent in Charge Harold Paxton would have one believe. In coordinating with U.S. Marshal Monroe Cortez, they had put Rosamund in the federal Witness Security Program and relocated her somewhere across the United States, other than Dallas, believing she would be safe from harm. Long enough to testify against the hitman's employer, Simon Griswold. Well, think and think again. That would not happen. As far as the assassin was concerned, the question was not if, but when he would fulfill the hit on the target for which he was being paid handsomely.

He was sure it would be sooner than later. Rosamund Santiago may be living under a different name to try to escape her all but certain fate, but he was undeterred. The hitman was methodical in tracking down those slated for death. His very reputation depended upon finishing every job he started. That meant following every lead and turning over any stones that would point him in the right direction. *Enjoy hiding out, Agent Santiago, for as long as you can*, the hitman thought, feeling the adrenaline rush that came with the hunt before the kill. When it was over, Rosamund Santiago would be dead like her late HSI partner, Johnnie Langford. And with this, the case against Griswold would go away.

DETECTIVE RUSSELL LYNLEY sat in the well-worn tufted armchair at his equally weathered wooden desk inside the small office at the Weconta Falls Police Department. The office had been passed along to him eight months ago by his predecessor, Fritz Kowalski, who retired the day he reached sixty-five, while still able to go out on his own terms. Russell only wished he could say he'd taken the job under his own terms. Instead, his life and times had been more or less dictated by family heritage and misfortune. None of which he had been able to have much control over, if not for lack of trying.

His parents, Taylor and Caroline Lynley, had both been involved in the criminal justice system in Oklahoma, where Russell was born and raised. While his father had a career in law enforcement with the Oklahoma City Police Department, rising to the rank of chief of police, his mother left her mark as an Oklahoma County District Court criminal judge. When they weren't dispensing justice, his parents were raising four children, including one adopted. Like Russell, all would end up following their parents' footsteps into law enforcement.

Russell was the third oldest sibling, behind Scott and Madison, and just ahead of Annette. After graduating from the University of Oklahoma with a Master of Science in Criminal Justice, Russell chose to go Scott's route in joining the FBI, becoming a special agent. Two years ago, he had been based in St. Louis, Missouri, enjoying the good life with his college sweetheart turned wife, Victoria, and their seven-year-old daughter, Daisy. Then unimaginable disaster struck. A brazen daytime home invasion left his wife and daughter dead, devastating Russell. Though the culprits were apprehended, tried, and convicted, before being sent to prison for the rest of their disgusting lives, the violent victimization left its mark on his life, coming so soon after the death of Russell's parents two years earlier in a car crash. Losing Victoria and Daisy had shaken his faith in human nature and the laws of morality.

Feeling empty and disillusioned, Russell quit his job with the Bureau. In spite of the support of his siblings, who had always been there for him, it simply wasn't enough. Wanting to seek a new direction in his life, he landed a job with the Weconta Falls PD as a senior detective and had settled, more or less, into a life in the small town in Northern California. While he wouldn't go so far as to say it was a crime-free atmosphere—there were the occasional murders, attempted murders, and other crimes of violence— much of the criminal activity was nonviolent or juveniles stirring up trouble to escape boredom. All in all, it was a nice respite from the big city crime and its consequences that he had left behind.

Though he would always carry with him the treasured memory of his wife and daughter, Russell had reached the stage where he was at least open to pursuing a new relationship, should it come knocking on his door and the pieces fit. Until such time, he was content to roll with the punches in simply fitting in and enjoying the things he did in his personal life, such as jogging, working out, reading, and relaxing to the sounds of jazz standards.

Russell was finishing up some paperwork on an investigation into an overnight shooting between feuding neighbors, leaving one with a non-life-threatening gunshot wound to the leg and the other in jail, when Detective Ike Wainright and Detective Gloria Choi stepped into his office. The two were partners and probably the ones Russell felt closest to on the force. Like him, both were in their early thirties. Ike was African American, an inch taller than Russell's six-foot-two height, a bit leaner, and had sable eyes and dark hair worn in mini dreads. Gloria was Korean American, a few inches shorter than six feet, slender, with long black hair pulled tight into a ballerina bun, and brown eyes.

"What's up, you two?" Russell asked, knowing they had been investigating a drug deal gone sour.

"We arrested the suspect," Gloria said. "Turns out the drug dealer was a twenty-seven-year-old unwed mother of three."

"Claims she only wanted to sell a small amount of fentanyl to pay the bills," Ike said.

"Did you believe her?" Russell asked, not that any excuse was justifiable for distributing illicit drugs into the community.

"Not really," he responded. "If she'd had her way, we'd be trying to locate more than a small amount of fentanyl, along with the meth and cocaine she possessed. But her buyer turned out to be a church deacon, who not only stiffed her, but turned the illegal drugs over to the authorities."

Russell grinned. "Good for him—and all of us, wanting to keep drugs off the street."

"Amen to that." Gloria chuckled.

A FEW MINUTES LATER, Russell left the building driving his official vehicle, a blue Dodge Charger SRT. While on duty, he was armed with a Glock 26 9-millimeter pistol, which he kept in a shoulder holster. He drove to a clothing store in the Weconta Falls Shopping Center on Tolton Way and took the statement of a clerk for an alleged shoplifting. Afterward, since he was in the area, Russell stopped by one of his favorite places to get a cup of coffee, Shailene's Grill, a block away on Liverwood Street.

He had just taken a seat by the window when he laid his solid gray eyes upon the gorgeous, dark-haired waitress waiting to take his order. The name tag on her beige café uniform identified her as Tisha. Giving her the once-over, he saw that she was appealingly small and around five foot eight. Her mid-length raven hair was in an attractive French roll updo. She had a square face and high cheekbones, pretty brown eyes that twinkled, perhaps even without her being aware, and a delicate nose. *Just the type of woman I could see myself with*, he thought, knowing full well he was putting the cart ahead of the horse. Not that the waitress was horselike in any way, shape, or form.

"If you need a few more minutes," she said impatiently, one hand on a narrow hip, "I can come back."

Russell colored, realizing he had been staring, a habit he usually tried to avoid, other than when interrogating suspects. He was fairly sure she wasn't a criminal in disguise. Yet, he sensed there was something more to the lady than taking orders for gawking men like him. "Actually, Tisha," he said smoothly, "I think I'll just have coffee, black."

She managed a smile and replied evenly, "One black coffee coming up." And with that, she left him wanting to know a lot more about her.

Chapter Two

In spite of her best efforts to the contrary, Rosamund couldn't help but check out the good-looking customer in what was her second full week as a waitress at Shailene's Grill. She guessed he was in his early thirties with black hair in a high and tight cut. He had deep gray eyes that she imagined a person could get lost in. An oblong face featured a broad nose, wide mouth, and a pleasing five o'clock shadow. Tall, with a solid build, he wore a business casual tan linen blazer over a navy cotton shirt, steel-colored khaki pants, and brown loafers.

Rosamund found herself trying to picture his lot in life. Businessman. Educator. Law enforcement. She wondered if he was married. Or had children. Not that it mattered. Knowing her time there was temporary, she wasn't exactly in a position to seek out someone to build a relationship with. On the other hand, as this was her current location and there was no one waiting back in Dallas for her return, she supposed there was nothing wrong with keeping an open mind. After all, wasn't that part of the requirements for the witness protection experience, to acclimate oneself to the community, as though one of its own? Except for the fact that, while in Weconta Falls, she was no longer Rosamund Santiago but Tisha González, she reminded herself. How long could she keep up the pretense before slipping?

Her eyes crinkled at the man who had just ordered black coffee, and she realized she'd been staring. "I'll just get that for you," she said quickly.

He flashed her an amused smile. "Take your time, but not too long."

She nodded, not wanting to keep him waiting any longer than necessary. Padding across the laminate flooring in comfortable slip-on flats, she put in another customer's order with Shailene McEnany, the fifty-two-year-old do-everything co-owner of the grill, before heading to the coffee station and starting another pot. Shailene, a breast cancer survivor, had bought the place a decade ago with her husband, Everett, and she was put in charge while he divided time between the grill and being a member of the Army Reserve.

"Keep it moving, Tisha!" Shailene yelled. With a medium build, her rose-blond hair was in an A-line cut. Her blue eyes widened behind contacts as she said, "There are other customers waiting."

"I'm on it," she told her and went about taking other orders in what had suddenly become a busy afternoon, before making her way back to the black-coffee hunk. "Here you are," Tisha said sweetly.

He tasted it. "Good."

She smiled. "I'll pass that along to Shailene."

A grin played on his lips. "I'm Russell, by the way. Russell Lynley."

"Tisha," she told him, even though he already saw the name on her name tag. "Tisha González."

"I know this may sound like a cliché or a line, but I haven't seen you around here, Tisha González."

"Yeah, that definitely sounds like a line." She couldn't help but chuckle. "As it is, I've only been working here for a couple of weeks, so…"

"Well, that explains it, as it's probably been that long since I last came in," he said, and laughed. "Anyway, nice meeting you, Tisha."

"You too, Russell." She found herself wishing they could talk more, as he seemed like he could be interesting, but duty called. "Have to get back to work. Shailene has no tolerance for slackers."

"I understand." He grinned at her. "Hope to see you around."

Almost sounds like he means it, Rosamund mused, but left it at that as she knew nothing about him and couldn't be too careful right now. She grinned back and went on her way. She had just delivered a stack of pancakes and a grilled cheese melt to a table and taken another order, when she was stopped in her tracks by another waitress.

Tracy Sheridan was a few years older and on her second marriage, with four kids between them. She was about Tisha's size. Her short, thin hair was brown with blonde highlights and parted to the side. Tisha felt comfortable with her as a work friend, almost on the same level as her friendship with Johnnie Langford. "Looks like someone has eyes for you," Tracy teased her.

"Who?" Tisha asked innocently, though in following the flight of Tracy's blue eyes, Rosamund guessed who she was referring to.

"The coffee drinker. Who else?"

Tisha glanced over her shoulder, while trying not to make it too obvious they were talking about him. It didn't seem to work, as Russell already seemed homed in on her and, with amusement, lifted his cup, as if in a mock toast. She looked away quickly, blushing, but curious about him nonetheless. "Do you know him?"

"Not personally," Tracy answered. "Maybe if I weren't already madly in love with my Milburn. Anyway, that's Detective Russell Lynley."

"As in police detective?" Tisha asked.

"Yeah. He joined the Weconta Falls Police Department about seven or eight months ago."

"Hmm…interesting." Rosamund had considered he might be law enforcement by the way he carried himself. Her instincts had proven to be correct. "Does he have a family or…?"

"Used to," Tracy said. "I heard he lost his wife and daughter. Don't know how. But apparently, he moved to Weconta Falls alone. I've never seen him in here with anyone, other than other detectives. So, I'd have to assume he's single. Especially by the way he's been checking you out."

"Oh, stop it," Tisha protested lightheartedly.

"I'm just saying." Tracy chuckled. "Don't know your relationship status, but if you're looking for someone, he might be a great place to start."

"I'm not looking for anyone," she said flatly, as though trying to convince herself of this. She hadn't been for a while now. And even if she was, it probably wasn't really a good idea to be interested in someone in law enforcement, like she was. Only she wasn't in law enforcement at the moment, consigned by circumstances to being a waitress while a hired killer was trying to hunt her down. Maybe it wouldn't be so bad getting to know Russell Lynley better, if he was truly interested in her, and see what came of it, if only on a temporary basis. When Tisha turned to look his way, she was disappointed to see that he was gone.

AFTER THE WORKDAY ENDED, Russell arrived at his single-story, three-bedroom, mid-century modern home on Drapmore Drive in a wooded area of Weconta Falls, still thinking about the attractive waitress named Tisha. Though only a few words had passed between them, there was something about her, beyond appearance, that captured his fancy. He hadn't quite figured out just what that was yet. Maybe tomorrow he would find an excuse to visit the grill again and see if they could talk longer than a minute or two. Maybe if she was single and available, she would even be amenable to going out with him. Or was his loneliness starting to play with his head? This was the first time anyone had gotten his attention even remotely since losing his wife.

Russell walked through the house he had purchased six months ago, attracted to its location as well as the blending of old with contemporary style, which suited him. It had an open concept with wood plank flooring in the living room and picture windows for natural lighting, a U-shaped modern kitchen with porcelain tile, and more than enough space for him to stretch out. He had outfitted the place with mid-century furniture and added a few modern accent pieces along the way. Still, he imagined it could probably use a woman's touch to feel more like home, but he'd learned to be content if he was to make this work, living so far from home.

In a corner of the living room, Russell kept a stack of classic jazz vinyl records his parents had left behind, along with a modern wireless record player. He pulled out a Billie Holiday album and set it to play on the turntable, then went into the kitchen, where he grabbed a beer from the stainless steel refrigerator. He sat down on a gray armchair and listened to the music while going over the events of the day, including meeting the new waitress at Shailene's Grill.

AFTER SPENDING THE next morning in court, testifying against a man charged with domestic violence, Russell headed to the grill, expecting to get another black coffee and more conversation with Tisha. He even sat at the same table as a sort of good luck charm. Only it was Tracy who came to take his order. "What can I get for you today, Detective Lynley?"

"I was hoping Tisha might be around." He spoke candidly.

"This is her day off," she told him. "Sorry."

Russell frowned. "So am I, but that's the way it goes."

Tracy smiled. "She'll be in tomorrow. But I would be happy to get you whatever you need."

He couldn't help but grin at the effort. Part of him wanted to ask her about Tisha, such as where she was from, if she was actually new in town, if she was single, and how she felt about dating a police detective. Stuff like that. But smartly, he realized that the best way to get answers was to ask Tisha himself. "I'll have black coffee," he told Tracy.

She cracked a placating smile. "Coming right up."

Later in the day, while driving around, Russell learned there was a disturbance at Weconta Falls Park. Apparently, some teenagers had been reported as harassing park goers. In Russell's mind, this was the first step toward the kids ruining their lives through escalating crimes that went into adulthood and gave them little opportunity to change the course before it was too late. He headed to the park and hoped to arrive before someone did something that couldn't be undone.

TISHA WELCOMED A day off to recharge her batteries. With Weconta Falls Park and its excellent running trails not too far from her townhouse, it was a great place to unwind. Jogging was one way she liked to do this. Though wary that a possible hired killer could be lurking about like a thief in the night, waiting for the chance to strike, Tisha had to believe she had been safely relocated. Protected and far from Simon Griswold's reach. As such, she was determined not to allow him to enjoy a moral victory of sorts by having her petrified at her own shadow. She still needed to have a life. Even if that life was away from work, family, and friends. She simply had to make the most of her situation until Griswold's trial and, presumably, conviction, at which point Tisha looked forward to reclaiming her life. She wondered, though, just what she would be going back to, with no one to come home to and cuddle up with at night. Would it really be enough to continue on with life as it was? Hadn't Johnnie's death proven, if nothing else, just how short and totally unpredictable life truly was?

Tisha ran down the well-worn path through a grove of ash trees and came into a clearing, when seemingly out of nowhere, she found herself surrounded by two, three, no actually, four persons. All looked like teenagers. Three male, one female. What were they up to?

"Hey, what do we have here?" said a tall and lean male with big blue eyes and a two-tone quiff haircut. He seemed to be the leader of the pack.

"No one you want to mess with," Tisha warned him. She did have pepper spray in the side pocket of her running shorts but didn't think it would be necessary to use. Not to mention her Thai boxing skills. Hopefully, it wouldn't come to that. The last thing she needed was to draw any undue attention to herself.

He sneered at her. "You sure about that, lady?"

"She's pretty," said the lone female, who was chewing gum and looked to be barely in her teens, with green eyes and rainbow hair in an edgy style with the sides shaved.

"Yeah, real pretty," said an African American teen, who was tall and lanky, and had dark eyes and black hair in a high flattop fade.

"I just want to finish my run," Tisha told them in a calm tone, smoothing her short ponytail. "I don't want any trouble."

"So don't cause any," said the other member of the pack, who was Asian and stocky, with brown eyes and curly brown hair in a brushed-up style.

Tisha frowned. "Go pick on someone else."

"Or what?" the leader of the group challenged her. "You're going to beat us up?"

While she weighed her options, having no desire to hurt any of them, but in no mood to be intimidated, Tisha heard a strong male voice that had a ring of familiarity state, "Maybe she won't, but I just might…" Tisha turned and saw Detective Lynley approach them. Where had he come from? He had a dour look on his face. "Heard some punks were stirring up trouble in the park," he said. "Thought I'd check it out for myself."

The leader suddenly seemed to shrink in Russell's presence, as though recognizing him, and uttered meekly, "We were just playing around."

"Yeah, right." Russell got up in his face. "Not cool to bully people simply trying to enjoy what the park is supposed to offer. You're lucky I don't arrest you and your friends on the spot and make an example of you for other idiots who like to play with fire but aren't prepared to face the consequences. I'll let you go with a warning this time. If it happens again, you'll all end up in jail. Not a nice place to be. Trust me. Now get the hell out of here!"

Tisha watched with amazement as the four scattered like scared rabbits. She faced the handsome detective, who asked, "Are you okay?"

"I'm fine." She met his eyes. "Thanks for your help, but I think I would have been able to defuse the situation on my own," Tisha told him stubbornly, though she was actually flattered that the detective had come to her rescue. She wondered what other damsels in distress he had saved lately.

He cocked a brow. "I'm sure you would have," he said apologetically. "Guess I should have mentioned yesterday that I work for the Weconta Falls PD. As such, after taking the call that some teens were harassing park goers, it was my duty to intervene—in case things got out of hand. Besides, I happen to know the father of the one I spoke to, who's a neighbor of mine. Whenever I can, I try to divert youths from entering the juvenile justice system, not to mention the criminal justice system, before they overstep and suffer the consequences that could last a lifetime."

"That's admirable, Detective," Tisha had to admit, knowing that she generally felt the same when she could use her own law enforcement skills and powers of persuasion to help at-risk youth avoid a life of crime and tragedy back in Texas. Sometimes it worked. Other times it didn't. "Hope it works. I'd hate to see them try that on someone else who might be packing. Or otherwise hit them back where it hurts."

"I couldn't agree more," Russell said evenly, studying her. "Kids will be kids, unfortunately. Sometimes they're misguided in trying to escape the doldrums of their lives. We'll see what happens. Or not." He was thoughtful. "I went by the grill today, hoping to see you there, but was told it was your day off."

"Yes, I actually do get one every now and then," Tisha quipped. She imagined that Tracy was only too happy to fill him in on the story of her life. At least as much as she knew. Fortunately, it wasn't very much, under the circumstances.

Russell laughed. "Same here."

"I'm working tomorrow," she told him, though suspecting he already knew this.

"Cool. But since I have you here, before I let you get back to what you were doing, maybe I could buy you dinner sometime, away from Shailene's Grill. Tonight, perhaps. Or whenever. If you're open to that type of thing…"

Rosamund sensed that he was fishing to see if she was single and available. She was, of course. But was it a good idea to even get semi-involved with a local, knowing that her real life was elsewhere? "Dinner sounds nice," she said, ignoring her previous thought. Maybe it was a good idea to have a police detective in town as an ally. Even if it went nowhere when all was said and done. Who said they couldn't be short-term friends? "I'll be free on Friday night." That was two days from now, giving her more time to get her stories straight in keeping up the necessary persona that had been created for her.

Russell smiled. "Friday, it is. Shall I pick you up or…"

"I'll meet you at the restaurant," Tisha tossed out quickly. She wasn't quite ready to share her address or cell phone number with him, even if she believed she could trust the detective. Right now, the rules of the game dictated that she needed to remain cautious about information she shared. Aside from the basics, most info was on a need-to-know basis. She was pretty sure that Russell didn't need to know things that might arouse his curiosity, causing him to pry and endangering her life in the process.

"No problem," he said. "What type of food do you like?"

"All types," she responded, knowing she was pretty much open to anything that wasn't too off the charts.

"Italian?"

"That works."

"Good. There's a great Italian restaurant on Kroper Lane called Italy's Corner."

"Sounds good," Tisha told him, grinning. They agreed to meet there Friday at six. Afterward, she resumed her run and found herself looking forward to her first date since arriving in Weconta Falls.

Chapter Three

Italy's Corner seemed like a great place for a first date to Russell. Or maybe it wasn't so much a date, per se, but getting to know each other better. At least that was what he hoped to get out of wining and dining Tisha González, who was not only hot as hell, but seemingly ready to rumble with some teenagers threatening her, whether harmless or not. This caused Russell to believe she was someone who was used to fighting her own battles. Was this a reflection of her upbringing? Or had she been a victim of bullying or another form of aggressive behavior that had toughened her up?

Russell couldn't help but think about Tisha's preference to drive herself to the restaurant rather than be picked up by him, the gentlemanly way. He wondered if she'd had trust issues with men in the past. Or was she merely erring on the side of caution, in case things between them took a bad turn? He would make sure the latter wasn't the case. As for the former, winning her trust was something he was happy to work on, if she let him.

When Tisha showed up right on time, she didn't disappoint in the least, wearing a body-hugging floral sheath dress and wedge sandals. Her hair was down and she looked great. "You look nice," he greeted her, downplaying just how much in his eyes.

"Thanks." Tisha blushed. "You too."

Russell grinned, taking the compliment in stride. He was wearing a plaid sport coat, with a peach-colored button-down shirt, brown chino pants, and boat shoes. The truth was, he was used to being viewed as good-looking, as was the case for all his siblings. Since arriving in Weconta Falls, more than one woman had made a pass at him. Though flattered, he had kept them at arm's length, not ready to start dating again. At least till now. They were seated at a table and had ordered white wine while perusing the menus.

"What do you recommend?" Tisha asked, as if he were an authority on the offerings.

In fact, Russell had only been there once before. But he was happy to share what he had then. "How about the chicken pietro and a combination salad?"

She smiled. "Works for me."

"Same here."

After the wine came and they ordered the food, Russell asked casually, "Are you from around here, Tisha?" He assumed she hadn't actually been living in Weconta Falls all this time. Though not tiny by any stretch of the imagination, it was still small enough that he would most certainly have noticed the striking woman at some point, had she been around.

She kept a straight face when responding equably, "No, I'm from back east."

"New York?" he asked curiously.

"Rhode Island. Cranston."

He had been there once on assignment for the Bureau. Small world. Would have been even smaller had they somehow crossed paths. "Long ways from home," he told her.

"Yeah," she concurred.

"How did you wind up in Weconta Falls?" It seemed a reasonable question to him.

She paused thoughtfully while sipping wine. "Things weren't going my way back home. I needed a change of pace. Made my way to San Francisco, where I had visited once. But that didn't do it for me." Another taste of the drink. "I was passing through Weconta Falls and, somehow, it clicked as a seemingly nice place to live."

"It is." Russell sipped his own wine, while pondering what things hadn't gone her way that caused her to want to relocate. A bad relationship, perhaps? Or something else? He gazed at her, interest piqued. "Thinking of settling into the town, are you?"

"Not so sure about that," she hesitated. "There may be some opportunities to pursue elsewhere. Right now, I'm just taking it one day at a time and seeing if this is where I truly belong."

"I see." Russell felt slightly disappointed that she might not stick around long enough to get to know. On the other hand, he admired her being candid about where things stood in her life, which he had to respect. Maybe the more she experienced life in Weconta Falls, the more she might want to stay.

After the food arrived, Tisha turned the tables on him, asking, "So, how long have you been in law enforcement?"

"Seven years," he answered pensively.

Her gaze held his. "And you've spent all of it working for the Weconta Falls Police Department?"

"Not quite." Russell sat back, holding his fork. "I was a special agent with the FBI for five years."

"Really?" Tisha reacted as though the notion took her totally by surprise, but recovered while continuing to eat.

"Yes. Up until eight months ago, I was working out of the Bureau's St. Louis Field Office."

"What happened?" Her voice soft.

"I turned in my resignation." He took a ragged breath. "Two years ago, my wife and daughter were killed during a home invasion."

"I'm so sorry, Russell." Tisha's eyes widened with sadness, but not necessarily shock. He considered that someone at the grill, such as Tracy, may have mentioned their deaths to her. If so, Tisha was tactful enough to let him tell her about it in his own words.

"It was horrible," he voiced, which had to have gone without saying, but he did so anyway. "The home invaders destroyed my life as I knew it then, and damn near my spirit. We caught them and they'll die in prison." Russell sighed. "Anyway, I needed to get away from everything that reminded me in a sad way of Victoria, my late wife, and our seven-year-old daughter, Daisy. So, I moved on and found work with the Weconta Falls PD. Not exactly bustling with serious criminal activity, taking nothing away from teenage troublemakers, but it's keeping me busy and has given me a new focus that I can live with for now." In so saying, Russell had to wonder if he was prepared to stay put any more than she was. Maybe someday he would re-up with the Bureau. Or find some other law enforcement career that could challenge him. But for the time being, Weconta Falls was where he wanted to be.

"I'm glad you've found a way to process your pain and stay in law enforcement," Tisha told him, forking some salad.

"So am I." Russell sliced the knife into his tender chicken. He was happy to feel enough of a connection with Tisha to share a part of his past that he hadn't very often since leaving St. Louis. Just as he was glad to learn more about her. Still, he sensed there were other things she was keeping to herself.

"What's your relationship status these days, if you don't mind my asking?" He assumed there was no one in the immediate picture since she wasn't wearing a ring and was having dinner with him.

"I don't mind," she stated without prelude. "I'm single. Never been married and no children." She paused. "Guess I've just never taken the time to go down that road. The fact that the right man has never come along to sweep me off my feet probably has something to do with that," she added with a defensive chuckle.

"Usually does." Russell grinned softly. He definitely wasn't holding it against her that she wasn't divorced, with children often caught in the crossfire of a broken home. While his parents had stayed the course in loving matrimony and parenthood till the day they died, he knew firsthand this wasn't always the case. Better for Tisha to have held off for the right man at the right time for love and a family. Russell considered that such person could even be him, if both stuck around town long enough to give things between them a decent shot to blossom.

After the meal, he walked Tisha to her car and Russell found himself eager to maintain the momentum he sensed was happening. "Hope we can do this again soon."

"Me too." Her eyes lifted to his. "I just don't want to rush into anything."

"No pressure," he insisted, even if a tad disappointed that she seemed to be holding back for reasons he hadn't quite figured out yet. "We can move at your pace. All I know is that I like you and spending time with you, though it hasn't been very much up to this point."

"I feel the same way," Tisha said genuinely. As Russell relished her words, she cupped his cheeks and planted a kiss on his mouth. Her lips were amazingly soft and tantalizing enough that, were it up to him, they could have kissed the evening away. But after maybe a full minute of their mouths testing the waters of compatibility, she broke the lip-lock and said breathlessly, "Thanks for the dinner and company, Russell. Night."

He thanked her and then watched as she got in the car and drove off. Savoring the taste of her lips on his, Russell headed to his own personal vehicle, a white Jeep Grand Wagoneer, feeling that things might finally be starting to look up after losing Victoria and Daisy. Yet he sensed there were still layers to uncover with Tisha, in spite of her ability to apparently downplay things, which in its own way made her even more compelling to get to know.

Is this really my best move, getting involved with a local detective? Rosamund questioned, as she headed home. Her lips were still tingling from the kiss she had initiated, which had been reciprocated in kind. There were clearly sparks between them. She supposed this had been the case to some degree from the moment they met, even if she had tried not to see it for obvious reasons. He seemed like a nice guy but may be looking for love in the wrong place at the wrong time. Was he truly over his beloved wife, dying so tragically? Or merely on the rebound?

I'm not interested in a rebound relationship, Rosamund told herself, nearing the townhouse complex. And she doubted that Russell would be much interested in her, if he knew she was not really a waitress named Tisha González but a special agent with the Department of Homeland Security, forced to hide her true identity while being pursued by a hired killer. Would he still see her as girlfriend material if he knew that, like him, she was in law enforcement in her real life and, as such, would always be in potential danger when on missions, undercover or not. Apart from being forced to lie to him, could Russell handle being with someone who, at least in theory, could end up dead and buried if Simon Griswold were to have his way?

It wouldn't be fair to put him through that, Rosamund believed, as she parked the car in the garage and headed toward her mailbox. Would it? Or perhaps she wasn't giving the detective enough credit for being open-minded and flexible when it came to understanding and going with the flow. Whatever that might be. After grabbing the mostly junk mail, she headed across the asphalt and was stopped in her tracks when she heard what sounded like rustling in the bushes. Though the parking lot was reasonably well lit, there were still dark places where, she imagined, a potential killer could be hiding.

There was the noise again. It seemed to be coming from a cluster of medium-sized juniper shrubs nearby. They were certainly thick enough and high enough to hide a human being, Tisha believed. Her first thought was that the hired killer had found her and planned to go on the attack. She did not have her firearm, believing it was smarter not to carry it everywhere in what was supposed to be a relatively low threat location. She did have the pepper spray, but feared it would be insufficient to stop a determined assassin.

She heard the sound again, only louder, as if to get her attention, if that hadn't been the case before. Just when she was about to demand the person reveal him- or herself, and while whipping out her cell phone to call for assistance, and at the same time considering making a run for it to her open garage door, Tisha watched in shocked relief as a raccoon burst through the shrubs and scampered across the pavement toward another set of junipers.

Taking no chances of further surprises, she raced into the garage, where she quickly pushed the button to lower the door, and then went inside the residence. She placed the code into the security system and then reset it to protect herself from any potential intruders. After sucking in a deep breath, she went into the kitchen and poured herself a glass of red wine. She tasted it and then had to laugh. *Guess I got carried away out there*, she told herself. The boogeyman turned out to be nothing more than a raccoon who was probably as startled by her as the other way around. Still, it reinforced just how freaked out she was at the potential for danger around every corner, so long as a hired assassin was intent on hunting her down like an animal.

Tisha drank some more wine while kicking her shoes off. At least she had found a sexy new friend, who happened to be a police detective and seemed more than capable of taking care of himself. Even if she was forced to draw the line at how much she could share with him about herself, she liked his company and he seemed to like hers. The fact that they both had experienced real tragedy made Tisha feel close to Russell. It also concerned her that neither may be ready to jump headfirst into something both might regret.

Her thoughts turned to the absence of family and friends in her life. And even her new partner, Virginia Flannery, who understandably had to be kept out of the loop for her own safety. It was easily the hardest part of being in the program. No goodbyes. Just gone like that, leaving others to explain for her. She didn't dare go against the rules and try to sneak a call or two, only to have it blow up in her face, with

Griswold's hired gun getting the bead on her as a result. *No, I can't make this easy for him*, Rosamund
thought, as she headed out of the kitchen, turned off
the lights, and went up the stairs for a nice hot bath
before going to bed. She needed to see this through
and stay under the radar until it was time to come up
for air and do her part to put Simon Griswold away
for good.

THE HITMAN HAD seized on some intel that suggested
the target, Rosamund Santiago, may have fled to
California. This, of course, would need to be double,
even triple checked, so as not to waste his time. After
all, time was money, and he aimed to keep as much
of it as possible for the day when he would not need
to silence people for his rich and powerful clients.
As it now stood, his inside source believed that the
U.S. Marshals Service pattern of relocation of witnesses tended to ship them out to certain areas of the
country relative to the original point of departure.
Seemed as though California was the preferred location for Texans needing to be relocated. But where
in California might the as-good-as-dead HSI special
agent be hiding? And what name was she going by?
When would he figure it out?

The hitman laughed at the thought of the agent
squirming in knowing he was coming after her and
would never stop. Until she was dead, like her late
partner, Langford. The assassin wondered if the

woman who shattered Simon Griswold's nose in multiple places, affecting his breathing and making him hate her all the more, would put up a fight against him as well. *Bring it on*, he thought. It was a fight she would lose. Over and over again. Unlike Griswold, the hitman never played by the rules. Except for his own. That meant his only objective was to get the job done, no matter who stood in his way. That included the target herself.

Rosamund Santiago may or may not be able to sleep at night. But she would know no rest for as long as she was alive. He would see to it. When he located her, she would never see him coming. Not till it was too late and she had breathed her last breath. Only then would the hitman be able to present to his employer the necessary proof that the mark had been eliminated. And thus, the biggest impediment to Griswold's future in continuing his lucrative business of human trafficking.

The hitman set his sights on gathering more intel and strategizing, before the time came that he would meet face-to-face with his prey. With the expected result of another job well done for him. At her expense as a dead woman.

Chapter Four

Russell was in his office, bright and early as usual to start his day, making himself comfortable at his desk. There always seemed to be paperwork, interviewing witnesses, taking phone calls related to investigations, or department meetings that kept him on his toes. Not to mention the incidents that brought him to the scene of crimes and required his investigative abilities be put to good use. Though none of these things taxed his brain like when he was thrust into high-profile cases with the Bureau, he was sure this was where he was meant to be at the moment. Especially where it concerned meeting Tisha. He'd had a mostly sleepless night just thinking about her and the tender—well, maybe a little passionate—kiss they shared after he walked her to her car after dinner last night. Maybe he was getting carried away in thinking that one kiss and a meal could be the start of something special between them. She did say she wanted to take things slowly. He needed to abide by that and let this play out at her own pace.

But did that mean she would object to his dropping by the grill this afternoon for a cup of coffee, just to see her again?

That train of thought was interrupted when Russell's cell phone rang. He lifted it off his desk and saw that the caller requesting a video chat was his brother, Scott. Four years his senior, Scott was the oldest of the Lynley siblings and currently a special agent with the FBI, based at the Bureau's Louisville, Kentucky, Field Office. He had been trying unsuccessfully to get Russell to rejoin the Bureau ever since he left. Was this yet another attempt in that regard? Or was something else happening in the family that he needed to know about?

Russell accepted the chat invitation and watched his brother's handsome face appear on the screen. "Hey," he said to him in a friendly tone.

"Hey." Scott grinned sidelong. Like him, his brother had their father's gray eyes and prominent features on an oblong face. His thick black hair was in a comb-over pomp style with an edge up and low fade. "Hope I didn't catch you at a bad time?"

"That depends," Russell half joked. "Was just finishing up some paperwork on a break-in. What's up?"

"Nothing nefarious," he assured him. "Just had a little free time on my hands after wrapping up a major investigation into a decades-old homicide that had ties to a current methamphetamine trafficking network and thought I'd check in on my little brother. How are you doing?"

"Congrats on solving the cold case," Russell told him, knowing this was his brother's area of expertise. "Me, I'm good." He sat back. "Keeping busy."

"So, you're not getting bored with small-town police work?"

Russell chuckled. *Here we go*, he thought. Subtle, if not direct, insults about his job. "Not at all," he told him. "As a detective, I'm kept in the loop for most of what goes on around here. While it may lack the serial killer, mass murderer, terrorist, or even drug-trafficking vibe I left behind, it's what I need at this time in my life."

Scott scratched his jaw. "I hear you, man. Seriously. You're entitled to grieve in any way you see fit." He paused. "I just think that leaving the Bureau as a coping mechanism was the wrong move."

"It was more than just a coping mechanism," Russell said. "I needed a change of pace. I found that here. I'm happy with my decision." At least for the most part. He saw no reason to second-guess decisions that seemed right at the time. He decided to throw his brother an olive branch, if only to keep the peace, but be candid. "I'm not closing the door on the Bureau," he promised him. "If I find myself burned out as a police detective, I'd certainly be open to returning to the FBI, if they'd have me."

Scott flashed his teeth. "You'll always be welcomed back into the fold, bro, if I have any say in the matter. Whenever you're ready to return."

"Thanks for having my back," Russell told him with a crooked grin.

"All of us have your back, Russell," Scott insisted. "That's what siblings are for."

"Works both ways." Russell knew he would always be there for them, as their parents would have expected. They spoke for a few more minutes, catching up on the latest family gossip, before hanging up.

Afterward, Russell finished what he was doing and conversed with some of the other detectives before heading out for lunch. He was eager to see Tisha again. The moment he stepped inside Shailene's Grill, his wish came true as there she was, busy at work. Russell wondered if she even noticed him as he took the same table he had sat at the first time he laid eyes on her. And once again, she was a lovely sight for sore eyes, uniform and all.

When Russell shook off another waitress, her spunkiness aside, making it clear who he was waiting for, he wasn't disappointed in the slightest as Tisha walked over with a big smile on her face. "Well, look who dropped in."

He laughed. "Hey, stranger."

She feigned disappointment. "Forgot me already, huh?"

"Not on your life," he told her seriously.

"Just testing you." Tisha chuckled. "Especially

since you chose to bypass another waitress for me and any tip you might have left her."

Russell chuckled too. "You're worth it," he insisted.

"We'll see about that." She blushed with a little discomfort, he sensed. "So, let's see…coffee, black, right?"

"Yes, that's right. But I also thought I'd have lunch today since I have some extra time on my hands." *That I get to spend in your presence*, Russell mused. He lifted the menu. "Do you recommend anything in particular for a hungry camper?"

"Hmm… If you're not in a hurry, I would go with the Shailene Special, which includes a nice-sized turkey club, fries, a glass of lemonade, and a slice of homemade apple pie," Tisha said.

"Sounds tasty," he had to admit. "I'll go with the Shailene Special."

"Coming right up," she said.

"Cool." Russell flashed a smile, holding back on what he wanted to ask her till she returned with the lunch. He watched as she sashayed away and couldn't help but wonder if she had been waitressing before moving to Weconta Falls. Or was she taking a different direction occupationally, like him? Something told him it was the latter, though he had no idea how she made a living in Cranston. He supposed she would get around to telling him when ready, were that the case.

By the time the meal arrived a few minutes after

the coffee, Russell had gathered his courage to continue his pursuit of the lovely Tisha González, while being careful not to crowd her. "Here you go," she uttered, setting the plate down, along with the lemonade.

"Looks great," he told her. "Can't wait to dig in."

Tisha laughed. "Hope you're not disappointed."

"Never." At least not where she was concerned. Russell would reserve judgment for the meal.

"Good." She grinned. "Then I'll let you dig in."

"Before you go, Tisha," he said, meeting her eyes, "while we're in the spirit of good, if not great, food, I was wondering if you'd like to come over to my house for dinner tonight. I'm pretty good in the kitchen. Learned how to get around in there from my mother, who managed to keep four hungry kids and a hungrier husband satisfied."

Tisha hesitated. "That sounds wonderful about your mom."

"It's only dinner and conversation," Russell threw out reassuringly. "No pressure, remember?"

Her features relaxed on that note. "I'd love to come over for dinner," she said.

He considered the come over bit, rather than his picking her up, his preference in an old-fashioned style of dating. But he didn't want to pressure her into anything that made her feel uncomfortable. "Cool."

Tisha flipped to an empty page on her pad and asked straightforwardly, "What's your address?"

Russell gave it to her while wondering how long

it would take to exchange phone numbers. Or was there a reason why she was hesitant to give him her number? "How does seven sound?"

"Sounds good," she told him. "See you then. Now, I'd better get back to work before Shailene cans me for fraternizing with a customer too long."

He grinned. "We certainly wouldn't want that. I'll see you at seven."

Tisha smiled back at him and walked off. Russell dove into the lunch, while already counting the minutes when both of their workdays were through and they could have their second date, more or less.

ROSAMUND ONCE AGAIN second-guessed herself for accepting another date with Russell. Was she playing with fire by allowing herself to get closer to the detective, who knew her only under an alias? If one thing led to another, would she only be setting herself up for more hurt in her life, once the truth came out and whatever was between them ended up going nowhere? Didn't Russell deserve someone who would stick around for a while, at the very least? As opposed to only being in town till it was time for her to testify, before resuming the life she left behind?

But he did say it was just dinner and conversation, right? Did he mean it? If so, what harm was there in that? Russell seemed to need a shoulder to lean on and so did she. Friends perhaps with short-term benefits might not be such a bad thing. If it was, she would feel it. Instead, Tisha felt just the opposite. It somehow felt right to be spending time with him, even with the future full of uncertainty where she was concerned.

Rosamund mulled over these thoughts as she went about feeding hungry customers on a busy afternoon. She glanced occasionally at Russell, offering him a smile whenever she could squeeze it in, but making sure she didn't neglect her duties, having little time to spare. In spite of a serious departure from her life as an HSI special agent, Tisha had surprised herself somewhat in quickly getting the hang of waitressing again. It was almost like she was back in college. At least she had an occupation to fall back on, should the Department of Homeland Security no longer have a need for her.

When she glanced again at Russell, Tisha saw that his table was empty. Already she missed seeing his handsome face, but knew it wouldn't be long before they got together at his place.

"He left you a generous tip," Tracy pointed out. "You must be doing something right," she joked.

"It's all in the wrist action," Tisha joked back. "Good service usually makes for good tips."

"True enough." She laughed. "But something tells me the detective wouldn't care if you were the world's worst waitress," she said. "As long as you're open to giving him a shot. Are you?"

I hate to be put on the spot like that, Rosamund

told herself. She recovered and answered candidly, "Yes, I think so. We're having dinner tonight at his house."

"Oh, really?" Tracy beamed. "You go, girl!"

"Try not to read too much into it," she felt the need to say. "We're not rushing into anything."

"Nor should you," Tracy insisted. "I made the mistake of doing that the first time around. Took a second before I knew what I was doing." She giggled. "When you're ready to roll, you'll know it. Trust me. And if he turns out to be a dud, you'll know that too. But I'm not seeing that in the detective, who seems like a stand-up guy you can count on."

Rosamund felt that too with Russell. She just wasn't as sure the same was true in reverse, considering her present circumstances. "Right now, we'd best concentrate on catering to the needs of those waiting to be served," she reminded Tracy, who agreed as they fanned out.

After taking another order, Tisha saw that a woman was now seated at the table previously occupied by Russell. Only when she gave her a soft smile did Rosamund realize it was her handler with WITSEC, Deputy U.S. Marshal Leah Redfield. Though they spoke regularly over the phone, Tisha had only seen her periodically, with Leah believing the threat level for her current location as a hidden witness was low, thereby not necessitating 24/7 surveillance.

Tisha walked over to her and pretended she was just another hungry patron. "Hi there," she said coolly.

"Hi, Tisha," Leah said unevenly. "Can you get away for a few minutes to my car?"

Rosamund sensed that something was wrong but knew this wasn't the place to elaborate. But she also couldn't just walk off the job, and doubted Leah would want that either, seeing that it was through the deputy marshal that she got the job. "I go on break in fifteen minutes," she told her.

"That's fine," Leah said.

"In the meantime, do you want something to drink?" Tisha thought to ask.

"Yes, coffee with cream would be great."

A minute later, Tisha brought the coffee to her and Leah paid for it. "I can get some work done on my cell phone while I'm waiting," she said.

When her break came, Tisha walked with Leah to her car, as the handler asked casually, "So, how have you been doing?"

"Good," Tisha told her. "I'm adjusting to my surroundings."

"Great." Leah looked at her. "Making any friends?"

"A few." Rosamund could think of one person in particular, Russell, who she considered a friend. Two, when she counted Tracy. Then there was an elderly next-door neighbor named Marlo Monaghan who Tisha had become friendly with, and who reminded Tisha of her beloved grandmother.

"Good to hear," Leah remarked. "Blending in is important as part of this new life."

Rosamund didn't disagree, in spite of longing for the best parts of her old life, which she anticipated returning to at some point. They reached the vehicle and got inside. Only then did Tisha ask in anticipation, "What's happening?"

Leah remained composed as she responded, "There's been a development…"

"What kind of development?" Rosamund could think of any number of developments. Had the threat to her safety been identified and neutralized? Would she be able to get back to her life sooner than anticipated? Had Simon Griswold upped the ante in wanting her dead?

"Through exhaustive efforts, we've been able to identify the hired killer," Leah said stiffly.

Tisha cocked a brow with expectancy. "Who is it?"

"His name is Arnold Nishimoto," she said. Leah opened her laptop and pulled up an image, passing it to Tisha to see. "Nishimoto's a thirty-six-year-old Japanese assassin out of Hawaii. He's been linked to at least a dozen murders, with hits put out by organized crime syndicates, drug traffickers, foreign governments, and, in this instance, a human trafficker currently awaiting trial, Simon Griswold."

Tisha's pulse skipped a beat as she studied her would-be assassin. Arnold Nishimoto had coal eyes, a round face, and short black hair in a fade cut. At a glance, he seemed like an average person and not a paid hitman. She imagined that false facade was what made him apparently so successful and in demand by desperate criminals who wanted someone out of the way. "Sounds like a scary person," Tisha remarked uneasily.

"He is," Leah said flatly. "Unfortunately, he's proven to be rather elusive. Right now, we have no idea where he is, but we're using all the resources available to locate and apprehend him."

Though that gave her some comfort, Rosamund felt even more anxiety in being able to put a name and face to the person who wanted her dead. "Do you think he has any idea as to my location?" she asked the handler bluntly. "Or name change?"

Leah sighed. "It's highly unlikely," she stressed. "We go through extraordinary efforts to move witnesses to a location where they will not be easily found. And only a small group of people in the U.S. Marshals Service have knowledge of this. Including the new name you've been assigned. So, relax. Arnold Nishimoto has no idea where you are. I'm only passing along to you this new intel, which I'll email you, so you're kept abreast of the latest news relative to your being in the program."

"Thanks for letting me know," Tisha told her gratefully, realizing she was overreacting to the idea of an increased threat level now that she knew who was after her.

"It's my job." Leah closed the laptop. "Though you should carry on with your life here as normal as possible, it's still important that you remain vigilant to any and all potential threats to your safety—to be on the safe side," she said, in what Rosamund believed was supposed to be a comforting voice.

But what Tisha actually picked up on was that, despite downplaying the threat, it had made it even more real to her. Meaning she would be that much more stressed while awaiting either the capture of the assassin, Arnold Nishimoto, or the trial of his employer, Simon Griswold. Neither one gave her much comfort at the moment, as Tisha felt the need to look over her shoulder at every corner for anyone who might be coming after her.

Chapter Five

Russell was admittedly excited about the opportunity to cook for a woman for really the first time since he came to Weconta Falls. Not counting the barbecue he'd hosted for his police department colleagues during the summer. As it was, Tisha was the first person he actually wanted to try to impress in the kitchen since Victoria died. Moreover, he liked the idea of spending some alone time with her, as opposed to a restaurant or other public setting. Even if it didn't lead to intimacy, which he certainly wasn't opposed to, he respected her boundaries. If she felt like the connection needed to progress further, he was all in.

For now, let's just work on her palate, Russell told himself, wearing a linen kitchen apron as he prepared veal parmigiana, sautéed mushrooms, and chopped salad. He made some oatmeal cookies for dessert, in case she was still hungry after the meal. There was wine and beer to drink, as well as water, coffee, and tea. In spite of being a little jittery at playing host, he was ready to go. If he played his cards right, Russell imagined that Tisha would be inviting him over to her place in no time flat.

When she arrived, he could tell Tisha was a bit nervous herself. He wasn't sure if it was the company or something else. He tried to make her feel at home. "Thanks for coming."

She smiled. "Thanks for inviting me."

"The food's nearly ready."

"Smells delicious," Tisha said, dressed casually but with enough style to get his attention. He had little doubt that were he to ever get her naked, she would be even more amazing.

Russell grinned. "I think I'll put on some music."

"Sounds good."

He went over to the record player. "Ever seen one of these before?" he half joked.

"I have a time or two." She laughed. "My parents actually owned a few turntables over the years. But I thought they'd gone the way of the dinosaur," she teased him.

"Then I suppose I'm a Tyrannosaurus rex." Russell chuckled. "My parents left me and my siblings with a stack of vinyl records. Between my brother and two sisters, I was the only one who chose to keep and play them. Fortunately, they still have some retro record players around."

"That is so cool," Tisha insisted genuinely.

"Do you like jazz?"

"Love it. Especially Sarah Vaughan, Antônio Carlos Jobim, Ella Fitzgerald, Billie Holiday, and Frank Sinatra."

"Great." Russell pulled out a Sarah Vaughan album and put it on. The fact that Tisha was into jazz was yet another feather in her cap, as far as he was concerned. "I can give you the grand tour."

"Okay." Tisha looked around. "I'm liking what I see so far."

"Then you should like the rest," Russell told her.

When they got to the primary bedroom, he wondered if it might be too forward to go in just yet. But she did so on her own. She surveyed the mid-century furnishings, including a king-size platform bed with duvet cover and a barrel chair.

"Nice," Tisha said. "Very nice."

"Glad you think so." Russell had no problem lingering in there, but decided not to push it. "Well, the food should be ready now."

"Good, I'm starving." Tisha laughed. "Never mind that I spent much of my day inside a restaurant."

He grinned. "I won't hold that against you if you don't criticize my cooking."

She chuckled again. "Deal."

Russell admired her good-natured style that was a good fit for his own. Tisha helped him put the food and drinks on the beveled top of the dining room table with boomerang-style legs, before they sat across from one another in upholstered side chairs. The conversation seemed to flow freely as they discussed some of their favorite pastimes, with Russell telling her that he too loved to jog as part of his work-out regimen. He proposed they might run together sometime, which Tisha agreed to.

"So, tell me about your family." Russell was curious to get to know more about her background. "Any brothers or sisters?"

Tisha moved the food around her plate. "My parents are semiretired, living the good life in Florida," she said. "And I have one younger sister, Gabby. She's married to a doctor and has two children. They live in Nebraska."

"Your family's spread out across the country, like mine," he remarked, cutting into the veal parmigiana. "Makes it easy to rack up the flier miles."

"Very true." She smiled thoughtfully. "Did you grow up in Missouri?"

"Actually, I'm originally from Oklahoma."

"Do your parents still live there?" Tisha asked, forking a mushroom.

Russell reacted to the question in bringing a painful memory to the surface as he tasted his wine. "They were killed in a car accident four years ago," he lamented.

Her brow creased. "Oh, that's terrible," she gulped.

"Yeah." He twisted his lips sadly. "They never saw the other driver coming. No chance to say goodbye properly."

"I'm sorry, Russell." Tisha reached across the table

and touched his hand. "I'm sure they knew how much you loved them. Even if you were unable to express it at the end."

"You're right," he said. They had expressed this sentiment often enough while still alive to appreciate it. Russell gazed down at Tisha's hand. Her fingers were soft. He liked the way they felt touching his skin. He met her eyes musingly. "Have you ever lost anyone you were close to?"

Tisha paused, played with her food, and then looked at him before responding. "Yeah. I lost my grandmother ten years ago, but it still hurts, as we were pretty close." She took a breath. "I also lost a good friend recently. He left behind a wife and two children." She paused again. "Sometimes life sucks, but you do what you need to do to carry on."

"Sorry for your losses," Russell told her sincerely, realizing that he wasn't the only one who had to carry and process such pain. "And yes, we have to find a way to adjust accordingly, if we're not going to let it drive us crazy."

"True." She flashed him a tender smile. "So, how about a couple of those oatmeal cookies for dessert?"

He grinned and stood. "Sure. Oatmeal cookies, it is."

Minutes later, they had eaten some cookies, before moving over to the square-arm sofa in the living room with their wine goblets. Russell was playing an Ella Fitzgerald album. "So, what else would you like to tell me about yourself?" he asked her, sensing there was still more that Tisha was holding back on. Not that he needed to know her life story, any more than she needed to know his, from top to bottom.

Tisha sipped her wine ponderingly. "Nothing much to tell, really," she seemed to dodge the question. Or was he looking for something that wasn't there? Then she said, as if a lightbulb went off in her head, "Actually, I've always had a fantasy about writing crime novels someday. Don't ask me why. Maybe it's the culture we live in that just makes me think I could sanitize the worst of it and create some memorable characters mixed with mystery and intrigue."

Russell chuckled. "Sounds like it could be interesting," he said, then sipped his wine. "I say go for it. With my background in law enforcement, I'd be happy to serve as an advisor, if you like, in terms of giving verisimilitude to the plot."

"I'd love that," Tisha said. "If I ever do plunge into the world of fiction writing, I'll definitely take you up on that."

"Good." He smiled, believing this might be a sign that there was some type of future for them to build upon. It gave him an opening to put forth another question he was curious about. "Have you always waitressed for a living?"

Her lashes fluttered. "Do you have something against waitresses?"

"Not at all," he stressed, hating for her to get the

wrong idea. "I have nothing but respect for wait-resses or any other jobs where the employees have to put up with sometimes difficult patrons. Also, I used to be a dishwasher and maintenance man on campus, while paying my way through college, so I'm never one to judge. Just wondering if you ever pursued or were into other occupations, in getting to know you better."

Tisha smiled. "Yes, I have worked other jobs," she said easily. "In fact, before I moved to Weconta Falls, I was a manager at a department store. But the economy being as it is, they started laying people off, including me. I took the opportunity to go in a different direction, literally. The waitressing gig is only a temporary thing," Tisha stressed. "I don't see my-self waiting tables for the rest of my life, trust me."

"I do trust you," Russell told her, more than he had anyone in a while insofar as in a dating capacity. "But for the record, whether you choose to be a waitress or anything else, it's fine by me. I'm just happy to have been fortunate enough to make your acquaintance."

She blushed. "I feel the same way about you."

"Good to know." Now he was the one blushing.

They listened to the music for a bit, before mov-ing in for a kiss. The kiss made Russell realize just what he was missing in terms of an intimate connec-tion since Victoria's death. He was eager to see where things could go between them. After a while, Tisha pulled away and touched her swollen lips, then said,

"As nice as that was, I think I'd better head home now."

Russell thought immediately about her wish not to rush into anything. He certainly wanted more, but would not push her out of her comfort zone. "Okay."

They got to their feet and Tisha said, "Thanks for dinner. I'll have to return the favor sometime."

"Whenever you like, I'll be there," he assured her with a smile. Russell thought this was a good time to see if he could get something more from Tisha as an indication that they were progressing in this relationship. "Can I have your phone number?"

She blinked thoughtfully. "Hand me your cell phone." He did and she added her name and number to his contacts. Returning the phone to him, Tisha warned lightheartedly, "Don't share it with anyone. Otherwise, I'll have to kill you."

Russell laughed. "Duly noted. I won't share it with another living soul."

"Good." Tisha smiled at him. "Walk me out?"

"Of course."

It was a warm evening and the stars were out. They took note of the latter admiringly, shared one more kiss, and Russell saw Tisha off. He headed back inside, believing they had turned a corner in whatever came next for them.

Did I blow it? Rosamund asked herself as she drove to her townhouse, still feeling the strong sensations from Russell's kiss. Had she overstepped in open-ing up perhaps too much with him? What if this prompted him to do some digging and he somehow figured out she was lying about some rather impor-tant issues in her life? Would he think less of her? Or have even more respect for what she was doing, for all the right reasons?

On the opposite side of the spectrum, Rosamund felt almost certain she could trust him. If so, why shouldn't she share more with him when she had no one else to lean on, outside of official channels? Giv-ing him her phone number was the least she could do as a normal means of communication. She also knew that it would not reveal anything about her real life that would imperil her safety. But she now had his number as well, as he'd sent her a sweet good-night text. Having someone locally that she could reach out to, if needed, was important to Tisha. The fact that Russell worked for the Weconta Falls Po-lice Department didn't hurt matters any. She con-sidered that his own boss, Diane O'Shea, the chief of police, was privy to her being in town under the federal program, having been informed by the U.S. Marshals Service and Department of Homeland Se-curity as both a courtesy and as sensitive informa-tion in an ongoing federal criminal investigation. But O'Shea was not obliged to share this informa-tion with other members of the department, unless absolutely necessary. Much like the predicament Rosamund found herself in where it concerned Russell. She could only hope that once she revealed her true identity and the life she left behind, he would not take the secrets she'd kept personally, and would understand why it had been necessary. How it might impact their relationship, or the possibilities thereof, was another matter they would need to talk about at the appropriate time. Assuming things went much further between them.

Once inside the townhouse, Tisha locked the door and activated the security system. The thought that Simon Griswold's hired assassin, Arnold Nishimoto, could track her down unnerved Tisha. She had to be careful not to become complacent. Or let down her guard, with the threat real, as long as she was seen as a crucial witness in the federal case against Griswold.

She showered and went to bed, allowing her mind to relax somewhat in thinking about Russell and what he was starting to mean to her as a boyfriend or even husband in a potential relationship. Would he be open to a long-distance involvement? Would she? Could they get past her being two different people, while still maintaining one heart?

THE FOLLOWING MORNING, while having coffee in the breakfast nook, Tisha received a call in a secure communication from the HSI Dallas Field Office special agent in charge, Harold Paxton.

"I understand that Deputy Marshal Redfield brought you up to speed yesterday on the killer hired by Simon Griswold," Paxton said in the video chat.

Tisha nodded. "Yes," she said solemnly. "I know that a man named Arnold Nishimoto is gunning for me and has a long track record of killing people." The thought turned her stomach. "And that he apparently never quits till he achieves his objective."

"Neither do we," the special agent in charge argued. "We're hell-bent on finding this guy, no matter how good he is at keeping a low profile, before he can find you."

Tisha cocked a brow. "Can he find me?" she had to ask. "Isn't that the point of my being in WITSEC instead of being well protected by armed marshals or the DHS in Dallas while maintaining my job as an agent—to keep me safe and secure?"

"That's exactly the point," Paxton said sternly. "We need you alive to help put Griswold away for the rest of his life. Along with some of his underlings. Better safe than sorry, as it related to putting you in witness protection versus subjecting you to armed guards for months. We've taken all the necessary precautions to ensure that your location remains top secret. That means Arnold Nishimoto is not going to discover your whereabouts."

Tisha sighed. "That's good to know." The thought that he could show up around any corner and mow her down or murder her in another fashion didn't sit well with her. How could it? "It's bad enough that Griswold ended Johnnie's life well before it should have been his time to go. The last thing we need is for him to succeed in silencing me too, so Griswold can continue trafficking human beings for hard labor, sexual exploitation, and trafficking of illegal drugs."

"I understand how you feel," Paxton insisted. "We won't let anything happen to you, Agent Santiago." He paused and Rosamund realized he had erred in using her real name that in turn could cause her to mistakenly refer to it, jeopardizing her safety. "Just continue living your life as Tisha González for the time being and you'll be fine," he said, correcting himself.

Tisha forced a smile. She had been venting to her boss, though he had tried to reassure her that the only thing to fear right now was fear itself, as the saying went. "Thanks, I will," she told him.

"So, how's it going there anyway?" Paxton asked.

"It's going." Tisha sipped her coffee, which was now cold. "Doing my best to make my life here workable." She thought about Russell. He played a big part in making Weconta Falls more than just a temporary place of refuge. Leaving it—and him—behind was something she wasn't looking forward to. Even while at the same time, she longed to get back to her real life, .

"Good to hear." Paxton sighed. "If there's any

more news to share, you'll get it from me, your handler, or even the police chief there, if warranted."

"Thank you," Tisha said, while wondering if Diane O'Shea could wind up spilling the beans to Russell before she had a chance to do so.

After hanging up, Tisha made plans for the rest of her day. She wasn't scheduled for work till the afternoon shift. This would give her time to go for a run and maybe do a bit of shopping. She was thinking it might be time to invite Russell over for dinner, as she had intimated to him last night. He seemed more than amenable to the idea. Though cooking was not necessarily her strong suit, in spite of her mother being a great cook and her father too. But Rosamund was sure she could put something together that reflected her Hispanic heritage and would satisfy Russell. If not in the kitchen, then maybe elsewhere.

Chapter Six

Russell did fifty pushups to get his morning started and fifty more to get the blood pumping. Honestly, he was feeling pretty light on his feet these days, thanks to Tisha González showing up in town at just the right time, giving him a whole new reason for being there himself. He liked the trajectory of where things seemed to be headed with them. If he had his way, they would speed this up and get to the bedroom part of getting to know one another. But since she seemed to be hesitant about taking it to the next level, he would abide by her wishes, happy to have a shot with the beautiful waitress.

After the workout was done, Russell took a call from his adopted sister, Annette. She was only three months younger than him and the sibling he felt closest to. His parents had already decided they wanted to add another member to the family and taken the steps to make that happen when they realized his mother was pregnant. Russell was happy they had gone through with the adoption of the biracial girl, as he couldn't imagine what life would have been like if he hadn't had Annette to play with and confide in over the years.

He watched as she appeared on the video screen. Annette, now a Dabs County sheriff's detective in Indiana, was an attractive woman with pretty brown-green eyes and long wavy brunette hair parted in the middle with bangs that were chin length. "Hey, you," she said spiritedly.

He grinned. "Hey, Annette."

"What are you up to?"

"Same old, same old," he claimed, while knowing there was something different in his life these days. "How about you?"

She frowned. "We're dealing with a double homicide here," she told him. "A man and woman were found shot to death in a vehicle. Not sure if it's drug-related, intimate or jealousy type of crime, or something else."

Russell wrinkled his nose. "Sounds like you've got a real doozy on your hands."

"Tell me about it." Annette gazed at him. "Anything out of the ordinary on the crime front in your neck of the woods, Detective Lynley?"

"Nothing like that, thank goodness," he told her. "Just the usual alcohol and drug offenses, delinquent acts, a hit-and-run here and there, and the occasional violent crime."

She chuckled. "Sounds like I should transfer there as a detective, while also keeping an eye on you."

Russell laughed. "You're welcome anytime. I'd love to have my kid sister around to hang out with."

"Kid sister? Hey, we're practically the same age," she joked.

"True." He grinned back at her. "Scott and Madison will certainly agree that, as the youngest, we both had to take our lumps from them. Maybe one too many," he added lightheartedly.

"That's for sure." Annette laughed. "But we got them back too," she reminded him.

"Yeah, there was that." Russell chuckled, then waited a beat. "So, I've met someone."

"Oh, really?" She narrowed her eyes with interest. "Tell me more."

"Her name is Tisha," he said. "We met at the restaurant where she works and hit it off." He was happy to share this with Annette, even when Russell wasn't sure where the future lay with Tisha. Only that he hoped there was something there to build upon.

"I'm happy for you," Annette gushed. "It's about time you put yourself back out there."

"Yeah, I've heard that from Madison and Scott," Russell admitted, as if that was news to Annette. "Hasn't been easy to let go of Victoria, who was the first love of my life."

"I know. That should never have happened. But Victoria would want you to be happy."

"You're right." He couldn't deny that, nor could he fight any longer the notion of being happy. Even though he was a widower, he was still young enough to start over.

Annette attempted to lift the mood. "Can't wait to meet Tisha."

"I hope you get that chance." Russell grinned non-committally. "We'll see where it goes."

"Well, I have another call to make," Annette told him. "Speak soon."

"You bet," he agreed, and ended the video chat.

Russell took a quick shower and got ready for work. He still had Tisha on his mind as he left the house and wondered when they might get together again.

TISHA WENT JOGGING in Weconta Falls Park. Mindful of her previous run there and the encounter with some teens looking for trouble, she took a different route this time, hoping to avoid a repeat just in case they hadn't gotten the message Russell tried to impart to them. Thankfully, she had no one impeding her way or otherwise challenging her right to jog peacefully. Not that she would mind having Russell show up again to come to her rescue, even if unneeded. He did say he was a jogger too, didn't he?

But her romantic interest was nowhere to be found. Tisha wondered just how much they could make a go of it once she spilled the beans on her true identity. Would Russell really be game to date a Homeland Security Investigations special agent? Would he ever consider rejoining the FBI if it meant being able to have a relationship closer to her world? Or would this be expecting too much of someone who left the big city and its association with the loss of his wife and daughter in favor of the slower pace and less stress of a small-town police force?

As she ran down the meandering trail, flanked by Western hemlocks, Rosamund's thoughts turned to her deadly pursuer, Arnold Nishimoto. In spite of the assurances of Leah and Harold Paxton that there was little to be worried about where it concerned Nishimoto, Tisha was taking no chances that he could discover her whereabouts and come after her. Were that the case, she needed to be ready. She was. Apart from pepper spray, she carried a mini stun gun in the side pocket of her sweatpants. Moreover, not even trusting that to stop a certified killer in his tracks, Rosamund kept her Sig Sauer P320-XTEN 10-millimeter pistol in an ankle holster for concealed carry. If Nishimoto expected her to be an easy mark, he had better think twice.

By the time Tisha came out of the park to jog back to her townhouse, she had relaxed, believing there was no current threat to her safety. As she ran along the sidewalk parallel to Pragten Road, she decided to invite Russell over for dinner tonight. Based on their previous meals, she had some idea of what he liked to dine on. Or should she pick something interesting to cook and surprise him? While grappling with food choices, Tisha heard the sound of a young female child. She seemed to be crying out in resistance to something. Or someone.

When Tisha turned her head, she saw a girl, six or seven, with long braided blond hair, being dragged against her will by a tall, thirtysomething, thickset man with dark hair in a cowlick messy cut and a Hollywood-style beard. He was dressed in black clothing and intent upon putting the screaming little girl into the open door of a gray Range Rover Evoque SUV. Tisha heard wailing from elsewhere. She looked to her right and saw a thirtysomething, thin woman with a blondish, red-cropped pixie haircut racing frantically down the sidewalk, but too far away from the child abductor, while the woman pleaded for someone to stop the stranger from taking her daughter.

For an instant, Rosamund thought about not getting involved, having no desire to expose herself when trying to maintain anonymity in the face of a real threat against her own life. But as she was the last thing standing between the child kidnapper and his getting away with his prey, possibly to never see the child alive again, Rosamund knew she had to spring into action. The thought of what this monster could do to the girl once he had her alone, including use her for sex trafficking, caused Tisha to shudder, while steeling her resolve. She immediately removed her firearm from its holster and raced toward the perp and frightened child, while yelling at the kidnapper, "Let her go!"

At first, he ignored Tisha, still determined to get the girl into the SUV. But as Tisha neared the two, she repeated her demand vociferously, "I said, let her go!"

The man turned toward Tisha and glared at her, while still clutching the girl, and said defiantly, "Or what?"

She was now just a couple of feet away from the culprit and his captive. Aiming the gun directly at the kidnapper's face, inches above the child he was holding, Tisha made her intentions crystal clear. "Or I will shoot you," she snapped. "And I'm a very good shot. Now, for the last time, let the girl go!"

As the man took a moment to weigh his options, he seemed to think better than to test her and released the girl, who ran into the arms of her joyous mother. He planted his dark eyes on Tisha, who told him before he could even think about coming after her or making a run for it, "On your knees!"

"I don't think so," he spat, grimacing.

In a normal situation in the course of her occupation in law enforcement, Rosamund might have shot him for threatening her life by his presence and the fact that he had reached into his pocket for possibly a gun. But in this instance, knowing that by doing so she would only be inviting even more scrutiny upon herself, she did the next best thing to mitigate her exposure as much as possible. Before he could pull out a weapon, with lightning speed she put her gun away and whipped out her stun gun and placed it on his neck. When he fell to the ground in agony, his muscles involuntarily contracting, she was able to disarm him. Afterward, her nerves frayed and once again holding him at gunpoint, Rosamund called Russell to report the crime, while hoping against hope that the local media wouldn't make a story out of it. With her caught in the middle for all the world to see. Or one dangerous hitman, in particular.

RUSSELL WAS IN the office of Police Chief Diane O'Shea. The forty-one-year-old petite and attractive divorcée and former police chief of the police department in Redwood City, California, sat in an ergonomic executive chair across from him at her U-shaped mahogany desk. She had been appointed to the position last year and seemed to Russell to thrive in the job and was unafraid of having to make tough choices. He listened as she vented about the latest proposed budget cuts that the city council had voted on. According to the chief, this would lead to a freeze in hiring new officers, waning employee morale, and limiting the tools to fight crime. He had heard it all before, even on the federal level. As far as Russell was concerned, one had to play the hand dealt and act accordingly. Of course, he didn't tell this to his boss.

Instead, he listened and, once she was through,

moved on to the reason he had come to see her in the first place. "This probably comes at a bad time," Russell indicated, "but I was thinking that it might be a good time to step up patrols around schools in town."

Diane, who wore her long brunette hair in a chignon bun, batted blue eyes at him. "Really?"

"We've had reports of increased drug activity on and outside school campuses," he explained. "The greater the police presence, the greater the deterrence in drug dealing and use."

"I take your point." She leaned back in her chair thoughtfully. "I'll see what I can do."

He smiled, taking that as a victory of sorts. "Thank you." Russell's cell phone rang. He was going to ignore it, but when he removed it from the pocket of his pants, he saw that the caller was Tisha. Curious as to why she was calling him during work hours, he gazed at the police chief and asked, "Do you mind?"

"Not at all." Diane grinned at him. "We were done. And I need to check my own messages." She lifted her cell phone from the desk.

Russell took Tisha's call. "Hey."

"I just stopped a creep from abducting a child," she said tensely. "Since I'm currently holding him at gunpoint, you might want to get over here. Now!"

He got the location from her and said, "On my way."

"What's going on?" Diane asked after he disconnected.

Russell was already on his feet when he informed

her, "There's been an attempted child abduction. I need to go."

She nodded. "Keep me posted."

"Will do." He left her office and informed other detectives about the incident before heading out. As he drove, Russell considered how and why Tisha happened to be in possession of a firearm.

ROSAMUND HAD BRACED herself for the questions she might be asked in effectively making a citizen's arrest and detaining the suspect till the police arrived. She couldn't shy away from doing the right thing when confronted with a child abduction situation. Even at the risk of exposing herself for a hitman to discover. Now she needed to try to minimize the damage, if possible, by maintaining her cover as Tisha González, a Good Samaritan who just happened to be in the right place at the right time. And hope that Russell bought it, even if she hated having to lie to him. But with the case against Simon Griswold still hanging in the balance and her testimony paramount to convicting him of human trafficking and related offenses, what other choice did she have?

By the time Russell showed up, other law enforcement had arrived after a 911 call from a neighbor, taken Tisha's statement, and had the suspect in custody. He was now handcuffed in the back of a squad car, while his firearm—which Tisha recognized as a 9-millimeter Luger semiautomatic handgun—and vehicle were confiscated as evidence and part of a crime scene.

"Are you okay?" Russell asked as he put a hand on Tisha's shoulder, causing her to feel the sensation of his gentle touch.

"Yes, I'm fine," she told him, even if shaken up by the crime and what it could potentially mean for her own safety. They were inside his official vehicle, not too far from the two-story Craftsman-style home where Suzette Haskell and her seven-year-old daughter, Deena, the girl who Tisha saved from being abducted, lived. She was now safe and sound, which gave Tisha a good feeling, knowing just how much worse things could have been for the girl and her mother. As for herself, Rosamund had managed to avoid any interaction with the local press thus far, putting her true identity at risk.

"Okay." Russell lifted his hand from her shoulder. "Now walk me through exactly what happened."

Tisha told him how she was in the cooling down stage of jogging when she came onto Pragten Road and witnessed the brazen attempted abduction by the suspect, prompting her to take matters into her own hands. "I wasn't going to let him take her," she insisted unapologetically.

"I'm glad you were able to stop him," Russell told her. "But it was still dangerous to take on an armed criminal. He could've killed you."

"Coulda, woulda, shoulda." Tisha rolled her eyes,

though not meaning to be flippant about this. "The way I saw it, that little girl's entire life was on the line. In that moment, I wasn't thinking about myself so much as the real fear that she would end up sexually assaulted, sex trafficked, murdered—or all of the above. I just reacted on impulse like anyone else probably would have in my shoes."

Russell glanced at her ankle where Tisha had replaced her weapon in the holster. "How often have you been carrying a loaded firearm while jogging, or otherwise?"

She expected this question to come up sooner or later. Rosamund knew she had to tread carefully, while hoping not to arouse his suspicion any more than was already the case. "Since I ran into trouble, no pun intended, with bad guys back in Cranston," she said, which had some truth in it, though under a different context. "I didn't want to become another victim in yesterday's news."

"Do you have a permit to carry a concealed weapon?" he asked, gazing at her.

"Yes, I made sure of that after moving to California." It was something Rosamund knew was part of the setup in her relocation under a new identity, while maintaining her right and need to be able to defend herself from a known threat. "Between the gun, a stun gun, and pepper spray, which I also happen to carry, I used the stun gun to subdue the suspect," she disclosed. "I just want to feel safe. Even in a relatively peaceful place like Weconta Falls." She met his eyes intently. "Evidently, there are bad people who wish to do really bad things, even here."

Russell turned away. "Yeah, there is that reality," he conceded. "At least there's one less bad guy on the streets of Weconta Falls, thanks to you. Hopefully, he won't be able to make bail and see freedom again anytime soon."

I'm keeping my fingers crossed that he stays behind bars, Rosamund thought, knowing that was where child abductors belonged. "What do you know about the suspect?" she asked casually.

Russell didn't appear to give much thought to the question, which was legitimate enough even for a waitress to ask, under the circumstances. "His name is Paul Skinner," he responded. "Thirty-seven years old, he has a record for child sex crimes, as well as other criminality. Apparently, he spotted the girl playing in the front yard, lured her over to him, and then grabbed her."

"Thank goodness it went no further than that," Tisha stated, knowing that even the attempted abduction would likely be enough to trigger nightmares and maybe require therapy for the victim.

"Yeah." Russell waited a beat. "We may need you to come to the station in the coming days to make a formal statement as to what you saw and did, if that's all right?"

Tisha smiled softly. "Yes, of course," she said lev-elly. "Whatever you need me to do."

She was not eager to give herself more exposure for something unrelated to the crimes perpetrated by Simon Griswold. But Rosamund wasn't about to give Russell more reasons to want to dig into her past by rejecting his request. Even if she had been assured that her true identity would be tough, if not impos-sible, to crack while under the program.

"Good." He grinned sideways. "Can I drive you home?"

"Yes, please do." If she might have been hesitant for him to do that before, Tisha was more than happy to have him know where she was currently staying now. Not only was it a smart idea that he was aware of her location right now, but it was a good segue to what she had in mind for them this evening. "In fact, before this nasty business of attempted child abduc-tion occurred, I was planning to invite you over for dinner tonight. If you didn't have any other plans," she threw out, just to cover herself and any disap-pointment should he turn her down.

"No other plans," Russell stated without hesita-tion. "After I complete the investigation for today, which might be a bit later than my usual end of work-day, I'd love to come for dinner."

"Since I'll be working the afternoon shift at Shailene's Grill, that should be perfect," Tisha said.

He grinned. "Then it's a date."

"A date it is." She was happy to see they were on the same page on that front, deciding there was no way around it, they were dating. Even if not everything was out on the table where it concerned the details of her other life, though it was getting harder and harder to keep this from someone Rosamund had begun to develop feelings for. But coming clean prematurely could do more harm than good, she feared, while placing her security, and potentially his, in jeopardy.

Chapter Seven

Russell couldn't belzieve that Tisha had singlehandedly stopped a would-be child snatcher in his tracks.
When combining that courageous effort with her
willingness to take on a bunch of teen bullies at the
park, and being comfortable with a firearm, it was
obvious there was more to the gorgeous waitress than
met the eye. But what? She mentioned having trouble
with bad guys in Cranston. What kind of trouble?
Had this forced her hand in readiness to be able to
defend herself and others in harm's way?

No matter how he sliced it, Russell was sure that
there was a backstory to Tisha and how she wound
up in Weconta Falls. Perhaps she would divulge some
of it tonight at her place. Or if not, then soon, the
more she got comfortable with him and knew he
was someone she could trust. For his part, Russell
resisted for now the temptation to pry into her history, believing that to do so might undermine whatever was building between them. He knew intuitively
that she was definitely not a bad person and, as such,

he could deal with anything else. What he also knew was that he was falling for Tisha and he had to trust her as much as he wanted her to trust him.

He sat at his desk, reviewing the information they had on Paul Skinner. It irked Russell, the thought that Skinner had been preying on children in Weconta Falls. How many had he already victimized? Were any reported missing of late? Had they really gotten so lucky as to stop a child kidnapping in progress the first time around for Skinner since his last stint behind bars?

I'll even take being serendipitous if it means saving a minor from the victimization brought about by the likes of Paul Skinner and others who perpetrated such heinous acts, Russell thought. He was still pondering this when Detective Gloria Choi came into the office with news.

"We have information that Paul Skinner may have been hanging around Loraina Elementary School the other day, before he tried to abduct the Haskell child," she said. "A car matching the description of Skinner's Range Rover Evoque was seen parked outside the school. There's even a report that someone may have tried to lure a girl going to school into the SUV."

"The pattern fits." Russell bristled, knowing that child sex offenders went from place to place in an attempt to snatch a child with the best chance to succeed in the disgusting endeavor. "We need to see if there were any other victims."

"We're looking into it." Gloria touched the fabric

of her one-button crepe blazer. "And also whether or not the attempted abduction could be part of a larger network of human traffickers."

"Good." He hated to think that human and sex trafficking was going on in Weconta Falls. But anything was possible. Especially when crime syndicates and criminal gangs knew no boundaries when it came to potential targets and locations for sexual exploitation. As such, why not Weconta Falls as a place for this type of activity?

"It's fortunate that Tisha González happened along when she did to prevent Skinner from carrying out his plan," Gloria remarked.

"Very true," Russell had to admit.

"Maybe we need to recruit her to come work for the Weconta Falls PD."

"Good luck with that," he said thoughtfully, even if it seemed like Tisha did have what it took to be a great law enforcement officer, starting with courage. Would she ever consider such, which would be a big departure from her previous occupations? "According to Chief O'Shea, budget cuts are coming, including a freeze on hiring in the department."

Gloria frowned. "That's too bad. We can always use more good people for the job."

"You'll get no argument from me there." Even so, Russell wondered just how much longer he would be cut out for detective work there, when part of him still longed to return to his previous job with the Bureau. Or was that simply a reflection of growing homesick?

"Didn't think so," she said with a chuckle.

"In the meantime, we'll just keep doing what we're doing and not get too distracted with decisions outside of our control," he told her, of which Gloria concurred.

AT WORK, TISHA was still rattled about the near abduction of a girl by a man who apparently saw an opportunity to grab her for his own deviant purposes. *What if I hadn't come along and been in the right place at the right time to come to her rescue?* Rosamund asked herself, as she juggled a hot plate with a BBQ beef brisket sandwich and fries and another plate with a garden salad and fish sandwich. She didn't even want to think about what that child might have had to endure had the perp succeeded in his brazen plan to take her. Tisha considered as well the horror the girl's mother experienced in watching the crime take place before her very eyes. She was surely second-guessing herself for letting her daughter out of her sight for even a second, while probably vowing to never let it happen again. If only that could be the case for all children preyed upon by sex offenders and traffickers. Rosamund knew all too well that prevention was only half the story. Arresting and prosecuting those who had succeeded in committing such offenses was the other half.

Tisha served the hungry customers, knowing that most had no experience being a victim of criminals of one sort or another. She hoped that would always be true. After taking the order for an elderly African American couple, Tisha looked toward the table where Russell normally sat. It was occupied by a burly, bald-headed man instead. She frowned but understood that Russell wouldn't be showing up today, as he had to investigate the attempted child snatching and build the case against the perp. Tisha looked forward to having dinner with the detective tonight. She hoped it would go well, even against the backdrop of the unsettling crime she had witnessed and immersed herself in, likely against the advice of her marshal handler, Leah Redfield.

THAT EVENING, RUSSELL had showered, trimmed the hair on his face, and changed clothing before heading over to Tisha's place. He stopped off at a store first and grabbed a bottle of red wine for his contribution to the dinner. He wasn't sure what Tisha had in mind beyond that, but he was certainly open for spending time with her in any way she saw fit.

"Hey," she uttered in a pleasant voice after opening the door.

"Hey." He flashed a grin as he stepped inside. "Brought wine."

"Thanks." Tisha took the bottle. "This will go great with the meal."

Russell smiled again. "Good."

"You clean up nicely," she told him, scanning his clothing.

"You too," he had to say, though unable to keep

himself from recalling how sexy she looked in the purple sports bra and tight black yoga pants she wore earlier with running shoes.

She blushed. "Thank you."

He scanned the downstairs for his first opportunity to check out her townhouse, noting the interesting layout and modern furnishings. "I like your place."

"It's not really my style," Tisha told him candidly. "But I needed something on kind of short notice and this was on the market, so here I am."

"I see." Russell wondered about the needing on short notice comment, as well as what her previous place looked like in Cranston. It only added to the mysteries of her life he still hoped to unfold.

"The food's ready," she said, heading toward the kitchen. "Hope you like Mexican?"

"Yeah, I love it." He looked at her, wondering if some recipes had been passed down to Tisha by her parents or grandparents. "Can I help with anything?"

"I've got it covered," Tisha insisted. "Relax."

Russell nodded. "All right."

Soon, they were sitting at a round solid wood dining table on white bouclé dining chairs, eating grilled chicken quesadillas with steak fajita salad and guacamole dip.

"It's delicious," Russell said, marveling over the food.

"Glad you like it," Tisha said, grinning, as she dabbed a napkin to a corner of her mouth.

He brought her up-to-date on the investigation

of attempted child snatcher Paul Skinner, and the likelihood that Deena Haskell wasn't the first one Skinner went after. "We think he may have been targeting girls at local schools," Russell informed her, "including Deena."

Tisha's brow creased. "Not surprised," she said. "He fits the profile."

Russell agreed, though curious about how she had reached this conclusion. Had she encountered child abductors before? Or was it merely guesswork considering the suspect's characteristics? "Yeah, seems that way. Glad we got him before he was able to fully execute his game plan."

"Yes, that is a relief," Tisha said musingly, and bit into her chicken quesadilla. "Hope he's put away for a long time."

"Me too." Russell stuck a fork into his fajita salad and hinted that they were exploring if there could be a wider network of child abductors in Weconta Falls.

She lifted a brow. "You think they could be trafficking girls here?"

"Doesn't seem likely," he contended realistically. "My guess is that Skinner acted alone. But, given the nature of the crime, we need to assure those within the community that this isn't a bigger problem that needs to be addressed."

"Makes sense," she said pensively, and sipped her wine. He noted that Tisha pivoted away from talk about child abductions to more personal things like family. "So, do you get to see your siblings often?"

"Truthfully, not as often as I'd like," Russell confessed, lifting his wineglass. "Between living in different states and everyone being busy with their respective careers and social lives, it hasn't left us much time to get together." He knew that moving to California had put him even farther away from the others, making it that much harder to see one another. But it also gave everyone a good excuse to visit his neck of the woods whenever they wanted. "How about you? Do you see much of your parents or sister?"

"I wish I could say I do," she said, a catch to her voice. "But I too haven't made the effort of late to bridge the gap between us." Tisha paused. "Hopefully soon I'll make the time to pay them all a visit."

"Or maybe invite them to visit you in Weconta Falls," Russell suggested. He assumed there was no bad blood between them or other impediments to visiting her.

"Yes, that's a thought, once I'm more settled in," she said, sipping more wine.

Russell wished he could get into her head, see what she was hiding from him. Or would that be too intrusive when he needed to trust his own instincts that whatever was in Tisha's past that brought her to Weconta Falls, he was grateful for her presence in his life. When it was time to get to the unknown aspects of her history, Russell was sure Tisha would share this part of her with him. Until then, he needed to take her for who she was. She meant more to him than anyone had in some time.

While caught up in his reverie, Russell had barely noticed that Tisha had stood up and reached out to take his hand. He allowed her to and got to his feet, whereby she started to kiss him. He kissed her back, pulling her into his arms, as their bodies molded together through the clothing.

"I like kissing you," Tisha murmured, while their mouths were locked.

"I feel the same way about kissing you," he told her candidly, and they went back to making out like teenagers. Or perhaps newlyweds.

"I want you to make love to me, Russell," Tisha urged after they had made their way into the living room between hot kisses. "I think you want that too."

"Definitely," he gasped. With his erection dying to come out in full force, Russell fought hard to maintain self-control, while knowing this was what they both needed from each other. Anything else could wait. "Let me make love to you, Tisha."

"Please do," she pressed, and led him silently up the winding staircase, down a short hall, and into the primary bedroom. At a glance, Russell saw a room with contemporary furnishings and an overhead wood ceiling fan with a light. He homed in on the white oak storage bed with a textured teal coverlet and fluffy pillows atop. Returning his ravenous gaze to Tisha, Russell uttered, "I'm eager to try your bed out for size."

"Be my guest," she challenged him enticingly. "So long as I'm in it with you."

"Wouldn't have it any other way," he insisted, and gave her another passionate kiss, before pulling back and watching keenly as she removed the spaghetti straps of her watermelon-colored tiered wrap dress from her shoulders. She allowed it to fall to the floor, then kicked off her slide mules. Russell took in her amazing body as Tisha removed her underwear and stood before him. "You're beautiful," he said, with her perfect breasts and the right proportions from head to toe. He wondered if she possibly knew just how gorgeous and sexy she was.

"Show me your body," she demanded, and he proceeded to shed his smoke-colored herringbone shirt, exposing his upper body. He dug into the pocket of his navy trousers and removed the condom he brought, having anticipated he might need it tonight. He tossed it on the bed and removed his Oxford shoes. Then came the pants and underwear. They were now both naked and at each other's disposal. "You are incredibly perfect," Tisha gushed.

Flattered but more enamored with her attributes, Russell cupped her high cheeks and laid another solid kiss on her ready mouth, before scooping her into his arms and carrying her to the bed. Tearing open the condom, he put it on and joined her atop the coverlet.

They went right into foreplay, bringing each other joy through their mouths and hands. Russell resisted going further, wanting to pleasure Tisha first, above his own needs.

When she apparently could not stand it anymore, Tisha cried out, "Please, Russell, don't make me wait any longer. Let's come together. Make love to me. Now!"

With this directive, Russell felt it was time to let loose. He positioned himself between her legs and entered her. As a primordial craving erupted inside, he made love to her, getting back as much as he gave, and then some. Their climaxes came quickly while exchanging passionate kisses. Afterward, they caught their breath and Russell knew Tisha was everything he could have imagined and more. Was this the beginning of what it felt like to fall in love again? Or was it too soon to even think that way, with some uncertainties Russell sensed were still swirling around them?

"YOU WERE INCREDIBLE," Russell whispered in her ear as if someone else might overhear him.

"So were you!" Tisha boldly stated as they lay side by side. She was still feeling aroused after climaxing with Russell simultaneously. The sense of urgency she had experienced in wanting to make love to him that night both frightened and excited her. The sexual chemistry between them from practically the beginning had finally caught up to her and, clearly, based on his bodily response, he was just as ready to take that next step.

"We make a great couple," he declared enthusiastically, while massaging her foot.

"You think so, do you?" Her voice was playful as Tisha enjoyed the massage, his long fingers magical in caressing her toes and heel.

"Absolutely. Or at least we have the makings of a great couple, if we allow ourselves to explore this and all its potential."

She felt a tingle at the suggestion. He had proven to be as skilled a lover as Rosamund had imagined and had given her another reason for wanting to be in Weconta Falls. If only to see through what they had started in what could become the incredible romance that had been missing in her life for so long. But was it realistic to think that this could actually go somewhere once her truth emerged? How would they do this? Was he ready to get to know the real her, beyond the real parts she had already shared?

Once Simon Griswold's trial had come and gone, Rosamund wondered if the feelings she had developed for Russell would sustain when she was no longer under a cloud of uncertainty and danger about the future. Wasn't it desirable and incumbent upon her to meet him halfway, if he still wanted her, and allow nature to take its course?

"There are things you don't know about me, Russell," Tisha hesitated to say, feeling she owed him at least that much.

"And you'll fill me in whenever you're comfortable doing so," he said understandingly. "I won't rush you."

"Okay." She left it at that for now, knowing that revealing her secrets might change everything for better or worse. Breaking further rules of the federal Witness Security Program might not only endanger his life even more, but could draw Russell into unwanted territory. Hadn't he left the FBI to escape the pressures he felt after losing his wife and daughter? Would it be fair to expect him to become ensconced in her own drama, Rosamund wondered.

She felt Russell's protective arms wrap around her, pulling them close in a warm snuggle and show of support.

So, Rosamund Santiago was now going by the name Tisha González, Arnold Nishimoto thought, as he gazed at the image of the special agent on his laptop while sitting in the front seat of the black Porsche Panamera Platinum Edition he was renting. No doubt she had altered her appearance somewhat from the official DHS picture. Perhaps she had changed the color or shortened the length of her hair. Maybe she wore contacts to change the color of her eyes. Or wore more or less makeup to disguise her true self.

Nishimoto had been sent the information from a

source within the HSI that told him what he needed to know to get the bead on the fed's key witness in the human trafficking case against Simon Griswold. To that end, Nishimoto flipped to another image and set of info on the laptop that had his attention.

Leah Redfield was the deputy U.S. marshal assigned to Rosamund Santiago aka Tisha González. Nishimoto studied the good-looking deputy marshal. He saw that she was currently operating in a Northern California town called Weconta Falls. Did this mean that Tisha was there too? Or a nearby town, where Redfield could easily come to the aid of the special agent and protected witness? He considered that if something were to happen to Redfield, there would likely be other marshals quickly dispatched to the area from the Northern District of California, with the aim of whisking Tisha away to safety.

"But not if I get to her first," Nishimoto said out loud. Now that he had a sense of where the special agent was holed up, it was only a matter of time before he made good on his assignment. He always finished what he started. His reputation depended on it. Tisha González was toast.

Nishimoto closed the laptop, set it on the passenger seat, and started up the car. He began driving while plotting his strategy for the death of the pretty special agent for the Homeland Security Investigations.

Chapter Eight

Tisha was busy serving tables at Shailene's Grill, feeling somewhat upbeat after Russell spent last night at her place. The sex had been off the charts, reminding her of what had been absent in her life. She wanted to see where this could go. More than that, Tisha felt relieved that Russell seemed to be willing to give her more time to come clean with the things she was hiding from him, albeit for reasons she was bound by as both an HSI special agent and important witness in the federal program.

With any luck, the trial of Simon Griswold would go smoothly with the expected conviction and then she could decide how to proceed with the rest of her life. She hoped that somehow Russell was able to remain a big part of it. In the meantime, she just wanted to stay close to him and maintain a low profile as an unassuming waitress and temporary resident of Weconta Falls. To that effect, she had phoned Leah Redfield yesterday to fill her in on the unexpected intervention in an attempted child kidnapping. Unsure how the deputy marshal might react to shining the spotlight on herself, Tisha was pleased when Leah seemed to downplay it as insignificant in the scheme of things. She believed it was unlikely the hired assassin would be smart enough or lucky enough to tie a small-town act of heroism to the HSI special agent and witness he was tracking.

That's good enough for me, Rosamund told herself, feeling relieved. She had been so preoccupied with her thoughts that she nearly spilled the caramel macchiato and chai latte drinks she was holding on a tray as she and Tracy came face-to-face.

"Hey," Tracy said, taking a breath, as she managed to hold onto a plate with biscuits and gravy, alongside bacon and scrambled eggs. "If you wanted to switch orders, all you had to do was ask," she quipped.

"Funny." Tisha laughed. "I figured practically bumping into each other was a good way to demonstrate dexterity in this business."

"Good one," she said with a chuckle. "I'll have to remember that. You can fill me in later on how things went with Detective Lynley last night," Tracy teased. "Right now, there's someone at his table other than him who needs a menu once your hands are free."

"Got it." Tisha didn't mind being bossed around a bit by the more experienced waitress who served as the assistant manager whenever Shailene wasn't there, which was the case today as she had a doctor's appointment.

After setting down the drinks, Tisha turned to the table where Russell liked to sit. She expected he might show up at lunchtime. If so, hopefully she wouldn't blush too much for all to see when thinking about their lovemaking last night. But sitting at the table was a tall, thin man in his midforties with two-toned hair color of medium-length, worn in a faux-hawk style, and a patchy beard. He wore a green crewneck T-shirt, relaxed tapered jeans, and black tennis shoes.

"How are you this morning?" Tisha asked him in a friendly tone, handing him a menu.

He ignored the question and stared at her with close-set blue eyes. "Are you Tisha González?"

Tisha's heart skipped a beat. Who was he and what did he want? The fact that he hadn't referred to her as Rosamund Santiago gave her hope that he wasn't working for Simon Griswold. Or with Arnold Nishimoto. Not that this gave her much comfort. She was feeling at a decided disadvantage. "Who's asking?" Tisha thought it best to use the direct approach.

"Name's Freddie Hildebrand," he said matter-of-factly. "I'm a writer for the *Weconta Falls Journal*. I'd like to ask you about the attempted child abduction yesterday on Pragten Road."

"I don't know anything about that," she claimed.

He jutted his chin. "According to a reliable source with the Weconta Falls PD, a Tisha González intervened while armed with a gun to stop Paul Skinner from abducting the little girl." Freddie looked at her. "I did a little digging and discovered a Tisha González worked here as a waitress. So here I am."

Tisha was furious that someone at the police department had decided to share her personal information with the press. She was quite sure it wasn't Russell. That left one of the other detectives or officers she spoke to. Her first thought was to deny she was the person the journalist was looking for. But Tisha was certain he wouldn't buy it, thereby putting even more unwanted attention on her. So she decided her best course of action was to get this over with and try to minimize the damage. Then it occurred to her that he might not be who he claimed. Mindful that his motives could be anything but pure, if not deadly, she asked him pointedly, "How do I know you really work for the *Weconta Falls Journal*?"

"That's a fair question," he said, and pulled his credentials from the pocket of his jeans. "Here's my ID."

Tisha studied it and decided it looked official enough. Still, she remained wary. "I'm a very private person, not looking for attention," she told him in a straightforward voice. "If you're looking for a story, you won't find it here."

"I just have a few questions," he persisted, "and then I'll get out of your hair."

She sighed. "As you can see, it's crazy in here, so I don't really have time for this."

Freddie picked up the menu. "How about if I order something?"

You don't give up, do you? Rosamund mused, her patience waning. "What would you like?"

"A Belgian waffle sounds good. And coffee with cream."

"I'll put the order in," she said. "Then you have two minutes, but no picture of me for your article. As I said, I value my privacy and have no wish to show my face and become the story. Are we clear?"

"Yeah." He flashed a grin, displaying dingy teeth. "Deal."

After clearing it with Tracy, Tisha brought the waffle and coffee and sat across from him. "So, what would you like to know?" she asked tensely.

Freddie spread hot butter across the waffle and covered it with syrup. "How were you so courageous in taking on an armed child kidnapper in broad daylight?"

"I only did what any law-abiding citizen would do," Tisha said, seeking to downplay it, "when faced with that situation. It was really no big deal."

"Most would say it was a very big deal," he argued. "If you hadn't come along when you did, the outcome for that kid might have been a lot different."

Tisha didn't doubt that one bit, imagining what she would have gone through had it been her own daughter targeted by a child snatcher. "I'm just glad I could help her," she said evenly.

"Yeah, about that…" Freddie dug his fork into the waffle. "Do you normally carry a concealed weapon?"

He favored her with a curious look, and Tisha could almost see the wheels turning as he wondered if there was more to her simple life than it appeared. She had to keep him at bay. "I like to when I'm out running, for self-defense," she told him smoothly. "I usually feel safe but know that there are those who might target women or children by themselves." She drew a breath. "Sometimes having a gun is the only way to get past the danger."

He nodded. "Sure worked this time for one little victim."

"Yes," Tisha said simply. "Well, I have to get back to work." She rose. "Enjoy the rest of your meal."

"Thanks, I will." Freddie smiled. "And thanks for stepping up and stopping that creep. Not everyone would have gotten involved."

Tisha acknowledged this much. "Just did what I had to." She walked away, while hoping this would be the end of it as far as drawing attention.

Tracy came up to her and asked, curiosity dotting her face, "So, what was that all about?"

Meeting her gaze, Tisha answered as honestly as she could without blowing her cover. "Nipping a potential problem in the bud." She left it at that while moving on to another table.

RUSSELL SAT IN his office and placed a video call on the laptop with his sister, Madison. A year and a half older, Madison was a U.S. law enforcement park ranger, working in the state parks system of North Carolina. Her attractive face appeared, which reminded him of their mother, including the bold turquoise eyes. Madison's blond hair was stylish in a shaggy wolf cut with curly bangs. "Hey," he greeted her, smiling.

"Hey, Russell." She smiled back, showing her straight, white teeth. "Nice surprise."

"Been meaning to call," Russell said guiltily, knowing she reached out more often than he did.

"It's cool, really," she assured him. "I'll take calls from my brothers and sister whenever I can, short of visits both ways."

"We'll have to try to get together for Christmas." He recalled the holiday was always a family favorite when their parents were still alive. It was even more fulfilling when Victoria and Daisy were still in the picture.

"I'd love that," Madison said. She ran a finger across a thin brow. "I'm sure Scott and Annette feel the same." She waited a beat. "So, would you be bringing the new lady in your life?"

Russell smiled, knowing he had yet to spill the beans to her, though not deliberately. "New lady?" he played along.

"Annette mentioned you had started seeing someone," Madison said. "I think she said her name was Tisha?"

"Yeah, that's right." Russell grinned, thinking about the amazing night they spent together and the endless possibilities that suddenly presented themselves for the future as a consequence. "We're not quite at the point of making plans for Christmas this year, but things do seem to be looking up for me in the romance category."

Madison's face lit. "That's wonderful. Can't say the same, but I'm always optimistic."

"You should be," he reassured her, knowing about the recent breakup with her boyfriend. "You're a great catch. There's someone out there for you, sis."

"Always nice to have my siblings there, even if from afar, to feed my ego," she uttered, chuckling. "We'll see what happens. In the meantime, it's ranger business as usual." Russell listened as she talked about her latest case involving suspected gang activity and drug abuse. "Seems like it's becoming a real problem around here of late," Madison complained.

"It's becoming a problem everywhere." He thought about the drug activity at schools in Weconta Falls, with a likely gang component. Not to mention the child abductor arrestee suspected of targeting local schoolchildren and the broader possibility that child sex trafficking could be an issue that bore further investigation. It was all the more reason that the police chief needed to step up in increasing patrols and surveillance in and around schools.

"I'm sure," his sister concurred with a frown.

Just as he was about to mention how Tisha had rescued a girl from victimization, giving him another reason to admire her strength in character, Russell was interrupted when Detective Ike Wainright knocked on his door and then opened it, stepping inside. The look on his face told Russell that something was up.

"I can come back in a bit," Ike uttered.

"Stay," Russell ordered. He gazed at Madison on the screen and said, "Sorry to have to cut this short."

"It's fine," she told him with a smile. "We both have things to do."

He grinned at her. "Talk to you soon."

"Promise?"

"Yeah, definitely."

"I'll hold you to that," Madison stated. "Later."

Russell waved goodbye to her and ended the video chat. He turned to Ike and asked attentively, "What's up?"

"Something interesting," he said nebulously, and walked toward the desk, plopping down on an armless vinyl guest chair. "Ballistics ran the 9-millimeter Luger semiautomatic handgun that Paul Skinner had in his possession during the attempted kidnapping of the girl."

"And…?" Russell peered at him keenly.

"Well, initially, nothing came up. Then the firearm and the ammo in it was entered into the ATF's National Integrated Ballistic Information Network," Ike pointed out, running a large hand across his mouth. "We got a hit. A confirmed match was made between the weapon and shell casings collected at a crime scene earlier this year in Atlanta, Georgia. The ballistic markings on the casings linked them to bullets that were in a gun used to kill a man named Earl Cummings at a party store, during an armed robbery."

Russell cocked a brow. "No kidding," he said.

"Turns out that those bullets matched test fired bullets taken from Skinner's gun where the barrel has a right-hand twist and five lands and grooves," Ike said, rubbing his chin.

"So, the weapon Skinner had was used to commit murder," Russell said.

"Yeah, that's about the size of it. What we don't know yet is whether Skinner committed the armed robbery," the detective stated. "Or if he ended up with the firearm after the fact. We're trying to see if Skinner lines up with the robbery suspect surveillance video recorded at the time."

"If so, that would certainly help put him away for a very long time." Russell leaned forward. "Even if he didn't commit the robbery, we've got him dead to rights on the attempted child abduction. Along with possession of an illegal firearm." As far as Russell was concerned, if convicted on both counts, that would ensure Paul Skinner spent years behind bars. This would certainly be something Tisha would take solace in, given her heroics in taking the perp down. And if Skinner was responsible in any way for the death of a man during an armed robbery, he deserved to be held fully accountable for that as well.

HALF AN HOUR LATER, Russell got a call about a woman found dead in a vehicle under suspicious circumstances. He headed to the scene, a warehouse district in downtown Weconta Falls, the attempted child abductor and possible armed robber and killer Paul Skinner still on his mind. Russell hated to think of what else the suspect may have been into. At least they had him in custody, thanks to quick and decisive action by Tisha, who deserved a medal, as far as he was concerned. That was on top of the fact that she was great in bed and great girlfriend material. He imagined she would make an even better wife and mother, were things to continue to progress between them.

When he arrived at his destination on Breckton Street, Russell got out and mentally prepared himself for whatever might present itself in this latest investigation. The decedent's car, a red Buick Encore, was parked haphazardly outside a building under construction. Detective Gloria Choi approached Russell. "So, what do we have?" he asked.

"A white female is dead, the apparent victim of a self-inflicted gunshot wound to the head." Gloria creased her brow. "An elderly married couple, Edward and Ruth Davidson, were walking their dog when they spotted the irregularly parked vehicle and grew suspicious enough to check it out. That's when they discovered the victim in the front seat and called 911. I checked for a pulse." She shook her head forlornly to indicate there wasn't one.

Russell walked up to the car on the driver's side. The door was already open. He eyed the decedent, who was slumped over the steering wheel. She was slender and looked to be in her thirties, with red hair in a pixie bob. There was blood on her beige twill blazer and dark cigarette jeans worn with pointed toe booties. On the floor of the car was what looked to be a Glock 27 .40 S&W caliber pistol.

Donning a pair of nitrile gloves, Russell carefully reached over the decedent to the leather bag on the seat and dug out her wallet. He lifted an ID and raised a brow when stating uncomfortably, "The victim's name is Leah Redfield. She's a deputy U.S. marshal."

"Hmm…" Gloria moaned. "Why would a deputy U.S. marshal take her own life?"

"Good question," Russell said. The Crime Scene Investigation Unit arrived, as was standard procedure in what Russell saw as a suspicious death. The medical examiner, Doctor Jessalyn Zegler, also arrived. A petite woman in her early forties, she had mid-length brown hair worn in space buns and blue eyes behind gray browline glasses. After a preliminary examination of the victim, Dr. Zegler said somberly, "The decedent likely died from what appears to be a self-inflicted gunshot wound to the right side of the head, causing massive damage inside."

Russell grimaced at the thought. "Any indication that drugs might have been involved in her death?" He considered depression or the stress of her job for the U.S. Marshals Service, similar to other types of pressure-packed roles in law enforcement, as possibly playing a role in the suicide. Assuming it was a suicide, which troubled him somewhat. Most of those in federal law enforcement, he believed, were thick-skinned, even amid adversity. At least where it concerned taking one's own life. Had Redfield gone against the grain? Or was it made to look like it?

"I certainly wouldn't rule out the presence of alcohol or drugs in the victim's system that may have contributed to her death," the medical examiner replied. "We'll know more once the toxicology report comes in."

As the body bag was headed to the morgue, Gloria said to Russell with a catch in her voice, "I've got something interesting you might want to see, Lynley…"

He turned away from surveying the surroundings, while wondering why the deputy marshal would choose this location to off herself, to find Gloria holding in gloved hands an evidence bag containing the deputy marshal's cell phone. "What is it?"

"Seems like Leah Redfield made a number of calls recently to one number," Gloria began. "It belongs to Tisha González."

A brow shot up as Russell said with shock, "Tisha?"

"Right. The very same Tisha González who saved the day in stopping Paul Skinner from abducting a seven-year-old girl." Gloria batted her lashes. "Looks like there's more to unpack with this Tisha than at first glance."

He was inclined to agree, as Russell couldn't help but think that the woman he'd made love to last night, and again in the wee hours of the morning, had some explaining to do. He wondered if it would change the nature of everything he thought they had going for them.

Chapter Nine

Tisha was happy to be home after a busy day on her feet at Shailene's Grill. She had forgotten over the years just how exhausting it could be, waiting on hungry and demanding customers at a restaurant. She thought about talking to the writer, Freddie Hildebrand, about preventing a child snatching. Though she could do without the attention and was still perturbed that someone from the police department had leaked her information to a member of the press, Tisha hoped the article might actually do some good in putting the spotlight on the dangers of child abductions, even in small-town America, the warning signs, and how everyone needs to get involved to one degree or another in order to prevent this from happening as much as possible.

Tisha had removed her shoes and liked the feel of the hardwood flooring on her bare feet. She imagined them being massaged by Russell, as he had last night. Might there be a repeat tonight? Or would it be better to tone things down a bit till more things were out in the open between them?

When she heard a car drive up, Tisha peeked out the blinds. She smiled when she saw it was Russell. Had he texted her to say he was coming and she missed it? Would he suggest having dinner at his place? Hers? Or a restaurant other than Shailene's Grill, knowing she spent enough time there not to want to use it as the setting for a date.

I'm open to whatever he has in mind, Rosamund told herself. And whatever came later. She opened the door before he could ring the bell. Grinning at him, she said, "Hey."

Russell was stone-faced in responding flatly, "We need to talk."

Tisha didn't particularly like his tone. What was going on with him? Did he have a change of heart about them before she got the chance to disclose the secrets she kept? Or did he have secrets of his own to reveal? "Come in," she told him. Only after he had whisked past her and she followed him into the living room did Tisha meet his unblinking eyes. "What do you want to talk about?"

"Leah Redfield," Russell said tonelessly.

Rosamund reacted to the name of her handler. What did he know about Leah? Had she confided in him about her situation? Should she even acknowledge knowing Leah Redfield? "What about Leah?" she asked tentatively.

Get Free Books In Just 3 Easy Steps

Are you an avid reader searching for more books?
The **Harlequin Reader Service** might be for you! We'd love to send you up to **4 free books** just for trying it out. Just write **"YES"** on the **Free Books Voucher Card** and we'll send your free books and a gift, altogether worth over $20.

Step 1: Choose your Books

Try *Harlequin® Romantic Suspense* and get 2 books featuring heart-racing page-turners with unexpected plot twists and irresistible chemistry that will keep you guessing to the very end.

Try *Harlequin Intrigue® Larger-Print* and get 2 books featuring action-packed stories that will keep you on the edge of your seat. Solve the crime and deliver justice at all costs.

Or *TRY BOTH* and get 2 books from each series!

Step 2: Return your completed Free Books Voucher Card

Step 3: Receive your books and continue reading!

Your free books are **completely free**, even the shipping! If you continue with your subscription, you can look forward to curated monthly shipments of brand-new books from your selected series, always at a discount off the cover price! Plus you can cancel any time.

Don't miss out, reply today! Over $20 FREE value.

Free Books
Voucher Card

YES! I love reading, please send me more books from the series I'd like to explore and a free gift from each series I select.

More books are just 3 steps away!

Just write in "**YES**" on the dotted line below then select your series and return this Books Voucher today and we'll send your free books & a gift asap!

YES

Choose your books:

- [ ] **Harlequin® Romantic Suspense**
  240/340 CTI GRSP

- [ ] **Harlequin Intrigue® Larger-Print**
  199/399 CTI GRSP

- [ ] **BOTH**
  240/340 & 199/399 CTI GRTD

FIRST NAME	LAST NAME

ADDRESS

APT.#	CITY

STATE/PROV.	ZIP/POSTAL CODE

EMAIL ☐ Please check this box if you would like to receive newsletters and promotional emails from Harlequin Enterprises ULC and its affiliates. You can unsubscribe anytime.

HI/HRS-1123-OM_123ST

He folded his arms. "She was found dead in her car," he said sharply.

"What?" Rosamund's voice shook. "How?"

"An apparent single self-inflicted gunshot wound to the head. There was a firearm found in her car."

"Oh, no." She put a hand to her mouth, disbelieving that Leah would have killed herself. Could she have?

"Your name and number were on speed dial on the deputy marshal's cell phone," Russell pointed out, making it clear he was aware of Leah's profession. If not her current mission. He peered at Rosamund. "Before I jump to any wrong conclusions, is there something you want to tell me…?"

"Yes, a few things." Rosamund's shoulders slumped. Under the circumstances, she didn't see how she could possibly remain silent about who she was. Not with him. "Where do I start?"

He sat down on an upholstered corner accent chair as he implored her patiently, "How about the nature of your relationship to Leah Redfield?"

Rosamund, her legs suddenly feeling wobbly, sat on the round-armed loveseat. She sucked in a deep breath, before saying candidly, "Leah is my handler with the U.S. Marshals Service."

"Really?" Russell adjusted his frame contemplatively. "Go on…"

"I'm in the federal Witness Security Program," she told him. "But not as a typical civilian witness.

I work for the U.S. Department of Homeland Security's Center for Countering Human Trafficking as a Homeland Security Investigations special agent." Rosamund paused, while giving him a moment to digest this. "My real name is Rosamund Santiago. Last month, I was working undercover with my partner, Johnnie Langford, on a human smuggling, sex trafficking, and money laundering ring operation out of Dallas, Texas. We were ambushed." She sighed as this was where it got hard. "I witnessed Johnnie get executed right before my eyes by the organization's ringleader, Simon Griswold. He tried to kill me as well and would have, had his gun not jammed. I managed to take out one of his cronies and get the jump on Griswold till help arrived."

"Sorry you had to go through that," Russell lamented. "And that your partner lost his life."

"Unfortunately, it gets worse." She twisted her mouth. "Griswold put a hit out on me to stop me from testifying at his trial on murder, attempted murder, and human smuggling charges, among others."

"So, they took you out of the field and put you into the WITSEC till Griswold goes on trial?" Russell ascertained.

"Yes, that's about the size of it," Rosamund confirmed. "I was given the moniker Tisha González, planted in Weconta Falls, and given a job as a waitress at Shailene's Grill. My only intention was to lay low till I needed to come out of hiding." She paused, gazing at him. "I never expected to meet you…and make a real connection."

"Was it really real?" He flashed her a doubtful look. "Or part of a convincing alias as Tisha González till it was time for you to pull up stakes and go back to your real life as Rosamund Santiago?"

Rosamund's nostrils flared. "That's not fair!" she snapped, even if part of her understood his skepticism. "Some things can't be faked. Not this. What we have…had…was real, no matter what name I was forced to go by."

"Dammit, you should have told me." His voice lowered. "Trusted me."

"I do trust you," Rosamund said honestly, but still needed to push back. "As an HSI special agent and chief witness against a major human smuggling operation, I was bound by certain rules of the game. Being a former FBI agent, you should know this. There could be no exceptions to the rule, not even you. Otherwise, I would risk not only endangering myself, but anyone else brought into the fold." Did he not get that? Surely he realized that this was bigger than the two of them?

Russell sighed raggedly. "You're right," he conceded. "You did what you were supposed to. I had no right to expect you to break the rules. Not even for me."

Rosamund was glad he acknowledged this. But that hadn't stopped her from wanting to do just that, more than once. "I tried to tell you last night," she uttered, "but you insisted there was no rush. To go at my own pace." She met his eyes. "Did you mean it? Or was that simply pillow talk in the afterglow of lovemaking?"

"I meant it." He held her gaze. "Whatever was going on with you, I never wanted to pressure you into filling me in before being ready to do so. Now I understand why you were holding back. I don't fault you for that."

Again, she felt relieved to hear this. Did it mean they could still have a future, once this was over? "Thank you," she said, pressing her palms together. "Just so you know, though, the U.S. Marshals Service did inform your police chief, Diane O'Shea, of my presence in town and alias under the WITSEC. So, it wasn't as if there were no active lines of communication between the DHS, USMS, and Weconta Falls Police Department in coordinating this effort."

Russell ran a hand along his jawline. "You played it by the book and that's the way it's supposed to be. Sorry if I made you think otherwise."

"Maybe I would have felt the same way, had the situation been reversed," Rosamund admitted, picturing it in her head. "I'm glad it's out in the open now." She frowned, while wondering how this would affect them moving forward. "I just hate that it had to happen with the death of Leah."

He leaned forward thoughtfully. "About that…did she seem suicidal to you?"

"Not really." Rosamund considered this. "I know she was divorced and hadn't seemed to be able to get the ex totally out of her system, but I didn't see her as being suicidal. She seemed to love her job." Which made Rosamund all the more uncomfortable with her handler's untimely death.

"Do you know if she used drugs?" Russell asked.

"We only met a few times and I never saw her take even an aspirin, much less any illicit drugs," Rosamund said. *Not that Leah couldn't have hidden this, as did many substance abusers*, she thought. Still, she had to give the handler the benefit of the doubt. "I think Leah was clean," she said point-blank.

"We'll see what the toxicology report reveals," he said. "In the meantime, the U.S. Marshals Service has been notified of Redfield's death. I'm sure a replacement handler for you is already in the works."

"I would hope so." Rosamund gripped the arm of the loveseat more than intended, while wondering if she had been made by the hitman, with Leah being a mere casualty in his way.

As if reading her mind, Russell asked, "What have you been told about the hired killer?"

"His name is Arnold Nishimoto," she responded, ill at ease. "He's based out of Honolulu, Hawaii, but apparently travels the world as a highly paid assassin. The feds are trying to determine his whereabouts and take him into custody."

"Hmm…" Russell uttered cynically.

"I can send you the info I have on him," Rosamund volunteered. "Nishimoto supposedly has no idea where I am. Or my new name, Tisha González." She paused. "But with the strange death of Leah Redfield, I'm not sure what to think."

"Neither am I." Russell chewed on his lower lip. He hit her with a soft gaze. "My brother, Scott, is an FBI agent. I'll ask him to see what the Bureau has on Nishimoto that might be of assistance. In the meantime, maybe you should stay at my place while we try to figure this out."

While she welcomed his show of support, Rosamund didn't want to make any sudden moves till she spoke with Harold Paxton, the special agent in charge of the HSI Dallas Field Office, as well as Monroe Cortez, the U.S. Marshal for the Northern District of Texas. The worst thing she could do was jump the gun and endanger Russell's life in the process. No matter his good intentions. She cared about him too much for that. "Thanks, but I should be safe staying here right now." She tried to sound convincing. "The townhouse has a security system, a good vantage point of anyone coming or going, and is where I'm supposed to be. Besides that," Rosamund reminded him, "I have a loaded weapon and am quite good at using it, if necessary." She also knew that she had her

Thai boxing skills as another means of self-defense.
Not that any of this necessarily ensured her safety
from a determined assassin, but she needed to keep
a positive approach for herself and Russell.

"All right," he acquiesced. "What about work? As
a waitress, I mean? In light of what's happened to
your handler, will you continue to work at Shailene's
Grill?"

Rosamund supposed it was a reasonable question. "I intend to keep things going as they are, until
told otherwise by the powers that be," she told him
straightforwardly. "A normal existence is part of the
program, unless there's a direct threat to that."

He nodded. "Just checking. Makes sense on some
level."

A thought occurred to her. "On that note, I do
have a bone to pick with your department."

"What would that be?"

"Apparently, someone there leaked my fake name
to a writer for the *Weconta Falls Journal*," she told
him. "He's doing a piece about the attempted child
abduction and was able to track me down at the restaurant for an interview. While I gave in and did it,
under the condition that no photograph of me was
to be used, I wasn't happy that my private info as a
Good Samaritan had been exposed, given that I'm
trying my best to keep a low profile for what you
now know are obvious reasons."

"Sorry about the leak of your assumed name,"

Russell said. "I'll look into it. Of course, if Arnold Nishimoto's none the wiser that you're going by Tisha González these days, it shouldn't be a problem."

"Hopefully not," Rosamund agreed, while reserving judgment.

Russell stood. "I have to go."

"Okay." Rosamund got to her feet as well. She moved toward him and wanted to give him a kiss, but didn't dare. She didn't want to make things worse between them by making assumptions that he still wanted to be involved with her. Or, for that matter, whether that would even be possible once her time as a witness in protection was over and done with.

Russell gave her a peck on the cheek and said tenderly, "Just be careful, and if you sense any danger whatsoever…"

"I'll let you know," she promised, grateful to know that at least he still had her back. What she wasn't sure of was if she still had his heart.

She saw him out, then locked the door and wondered uneasily what came next in what was turning out to be a potentially deadly game of cat and mouse.

RUSSELL WANTED TO kick himself for acting like a bratty teenager who had been left hanging at the prom by the prettiest girl in school. Well, maybe that was getting carried away with his reaction upon learning that Tisha González, the gorgeous waitress he had started to fall in love with, was actually Rosa-

mund Santiago, a Homeland Security Investigations
special agent and in the federal program. It was less
about the fact that she had intentionally misled him,
given that Rosamund had no choice really, but that
he had failed to discover this on his own as a former FBI agent who was usually quite perceptive in
unraveling clues that presented themselves. *Maybe
I didn't want to know that Tisha was anything other
than what or whom she pretended to be*, Russell told
himself, as he drove back to the police department.
Maybe it was safer for him to wear blinders so he
wouldn't be hurt again, as he was when he lost his
wife and daughter.

But didn't hurt come with the territory of living?
Would he ever be able to truly steel himself from
the pain of things being out of his control? He had
to believe that there really was something there between him and Tisha or Rosamund. She had as much
as told him so. He didn't believe for one minute that
the way they were together in and out of bed was just
for show. Rosamund had been put into a nearly im-
possible situation after watching her partner die and
being left to fend for both of them against a human
smuggler. Obviously, the DHS felt her testimony was
critical to putting away Simon Griswold. So much
so that, rather than risk her being killed after Griswold had put a hit out on her by having her continue
her normal duties as an HSI special agent, they took
the unusual step for someone in her position and

placed her in witness protection. In which case, they hoped to keep Rosamund alive long enough to testify against Griswold.

She had never asked to be temporarily relocated to Weconta Falls and pursued by a lonely police detective who found her attractive. Rosamund must have seen something in him that made her want to get to know him as much as he sought to get to know her. They clicked, pure and simple. Having a different name to go by and different circumstances coming to light wouldn't change that. The fact that, as Tisha, she risked life and limb by exposing herself to prevent a little girl from being abducted by a known child sex offender told Russell all he needed to know about Rosamund.

He owed it to her and himself not to bail at a time when Rosamund's life was in danger, with her being pursued by a hired killer who may have found his target. Once her safety had been assured and the business of testifying in court against a trafficker was over, they could decide where to go with their own relationship. If there was anywhere to go. He needed to be realistic about this, his own desires notwithstanding. They had both established themselves in their chosen professions in different parts of the country. He couldn't expect Rosamund to walk away from the life she had built and he wouldn't expect that she would ask the same of him. Russell knew that, no matter what, he would have to respect whatever happened. For now, the focus needed to be on doing what it took to keep a hitman from carrying out his assignment. To Russell, the idea of watching another person he had fallen in love with die before her time was unthinkable. Not as long as he was still breathing and determined to prevent that from happening.

Chapter Ten

After Russell left, Rosamund's cell phone rang. She saw that the caller was U.S. Marshal Monroe Cortez. She took the call nervously, as this was their first contact since she entered the federal program. "I gather you've heard that Deputy U.S. Marshal Leah Redfield is dead," he voiced somberly.

"Yes," Rosamund responded, as she stood in the kitchen. She felt saddened that another person in law enforcement she had gotten to know somewhat was a victim of fatal gunfire. "They think she committed suicide."

"That appears to be the case," the marshal acknowledged. "Though, an investigation is still pending."

"Why would Leah take her own life?" Rosamund questioned. "She seemed happy."

"We can't ever truly know what's going on inside a person's head, can we?" he said flatly. "Maybe Deputy Marshal Redfield was battling depression or other demons that she was able to successfully conceal outwardly. Till she couldn't any longer."

Rosamund wondered if the pressure of being her handler had been too much for Leah. But if that were so, wouldn't she have been able to pick up on it during their communication? "Maybe Simon Griswold's hired killer, Arnold Nishimoto, got to Leah?"

Cortez cleared his throat. "There's no indication that Nishimoto has discovered your whereabouts," the marshal insisted. "He's likely unaware that we're onto him and pursuing every lead in bringing him to justice. We think you're still safe for now."

Rosamund wasn't convinced that the assassin hadn't somehow made his way to Weconta Falls against all odds. After all, wasn't that the nature of this beast, eluding capture while successfully going after his own prey? "Will I get a new handler?"

"Yes, that's why I'm calling," he said, "along with reassuring you that the tragic loss of Deputy Marshal Redfield does not mean we'd shirk our responsibilities in protecting an important witness. Assigned to take her place as your handler is Deputy U.S. Marshal Patrick McDermott. I'm sending you his photograph now."

"Okay." Rosamund received the picture, studying her new handler. Patrick McDermott was in his midforties and biracial with curly dark brown hair in a low skin fade cut and deep sable eyes.

"McDermott is a fifteen-year veteran of the U.S. Marshals Service, based in San Francisco," Cortez said. "He has lots of experience in these types of assignments and will be setting up a meeting with you in the morning. Meanwhile, to be on the safe side, we've arranged for the Weconta Falls Police Department to keep an officer outside the townhouse and at your workplace for your protection till then. If need be, we'll relocate you to a different area to ensure your safety till Griswold's trial."

"All right." She welcomed the officer's presence but, truthfully, would have preferred to have Russell on hand, if anyone. But Rosamund wasn't sure he felt the same way, in spite of their seeming to have gotten past the strain that came from her true identity being revealed. As it was, she was prepared to defend herself from a known enemy if need be.

"Any questions?" Cortez asked.

Rosamund had none at the moment that hadn't already been addressed. What queries she did have would be addressed with Harold Paxton. And then she would go from there in an effort to stay one step ahead of danger.

WHEN RUSSELL WALKED into Diane O'Shea's office, the chief of police was clearly expecting him. "Sit down, Lynley," she ordered in a controlled tone of voice. He complied, taking a seat, while she leaned against a corner of her desk. "I understand that you and Choi are looking into the death of Deputy U.S. Marshal Leah Redfield."

"Yeah," he told her. "The medical examiner views it as a probable suicide."

"But you don't?" Diane seemed to pick up on this.

"It looks that way," Russell conceded. "But I have reason to believe that she could have been murdered. At the very least, the timing of Redfield's death is more than a little suspicious, considering she was the handler for a federal witness in a human trafficking case." He wondered if the chief would come clean on her knowledge of this.

Diane arched a brow. "You know about that?"

Russell met her eyes. "Yeah," he admitted. "I know that Tisha González, a waitress at Shailene's Grill, is actually Homeland Security Investigations Special Agent Rosamund Santiago, who's been put in the federal Witness Security Program while awaiting her testimony in the trial of suspected human trafficker Simon Griswold."

"But how?" Diane looked perplexed.

"In the days leading up to her death, Redfield made several phone calls to Tisha," he pointed out. "I recognized the name…" Russell considered whether or not it was a good idea to fess up on his involvement with Rosamund and how this might play with the police chief in moving forward when it came to keeping the witness safe. "Full disclosure," he said, deciding to lay it out. "I've been seeing the waitress whom I knew as Tisha González up until today. She brought me up to speed on her true identity, Rosamund Santiago, HSI special agent, and what was going on with respect to her association with Deputy U.S. Marshal Redfield and laying low in Weconta Falls till it was time to reemerge to testify against the reputed human trafficker." He paused. "Rosamund also told me that you were privy to her presence in our town."

"As the chief of police, of course I was," Diane acknowledged. "I called you in here to brief you after learning about the death of Deputy Marshal Redfield."

Russell frowned. "You might have given me a heads-up on the particulars before now." He realized she wasn't obligated to do so, but he would have liked to know they had a federal witness there to help protect. Never mind the fact that had he known Tisha, the waitress, was an alias for a DHS special agent, it could have changed the trajectory of their relationship. For better or worse.

"That wasn't really my call," the chief said, defending herself. "The U.S. Marshals Service was in charge of the process and didn't necessarily want us stepping on any toes by having too many feet in the game, so to speak. And the witness did not appear to be in imminent danger, as I was told, to necessitate a greater role in protecting her, beyond having a patrol car drive by her place every now and then. Besides, you had your hands full, Lynley, and didn't need any distractions."

Russell couldn't very well push back from that assessment, seeing that she was right. It wouldn't have been the norm to have him involved in protecting a federal witness. Of course, there was still twenty-twenty hindsight considering his relationship—if there was still one—with Rosamund. "I understand," he said respectfully. "So, where do things stand now in keeping Special Agent Santiago out of harm's way?"

Diane scratched the side of her nose. "A new deputy marshal will be sent in to be her handler," she replied. "In the meantime, at the request of the USMS, we've assigned an officer, Kevin Wilkinson, ten-year veteran of the Weconta Falls Police Department, to keep an eye on her."

"With Agent Santiago being targeted by a hitman, I'd like to be an extra pair of eyes in ensuring her safety while she's in our jurisdiction." Russell knew he was asking a lot of the chief, with a staff shortage and obvious conflict of interest, but he wasn't going to sit back and let an assassin have his way in taking out Rosamund.

Diane pursed her lips. "Getting romantically involved with a federal witness is never a good idea," she cautioned. "Even worse is interfering with a WITSEC underway."

"I know." He furrowed his brow. "But it is what it is. I need to do this," he insisted.

She held his firm gaze. "I strongly advise against butting heads with the USMS, as it seems as though they've got this." The chief sighed. "However, seeing that it was unplanned on your part to connect with Agent Santiago in the way you have, do what you need to while holding the line in representing the department in this assignment. Beyond that, what you do off duty to help keep Agent Santiago safe is up to you. Just be smart about it."

Russell grinned. "Thanks, Chief." She did have his back and, for that, he owed her one.

Diane nodded. "Good luck," she said, leaving it to him to interpret her meaning.

He went to his office, closed the door, and sat at his desk. The first thing Russell found himself doing was getting on his laptop to get a better read on Rosamund Santiago, for who she really was, as opposed to what he had been led to believe. In doing a general search for federal employees, he found her profile. Age thirty-two. Single. Born in El Paso, Texas. Attended the University of Texas at Arlington, where she received a Bachelor's degree in Interdisciplinary Studies and a Master's degree in Criminology and Criminal Justice. She went to work afterward for the Department of Homeland Security's Center for Countering Human Trafficking. Within this context, Rosamund became a Homeland Security Investigations special agent, receiving commendations for her efforts in taking down human traffickers and their networks.

All in all, Russell couldn't help but be impressed

by the special agent. Obviously, she was doing something good with her life that she should be proud of. He once felt that way when he was with the Bureau. Till faced with the type of tragedy he wouldn't wish upon his worst enemy, causing him to retreat.

He brought up an article on the human trafficking operation she was involved in that took the life of her partner, Special Agent Johnnie Langford. Rosamund barely survived. Russell winced at the thought of not having the opportunity to meet Tisha, aka Rosamund, were it not for the unlikelihood of a gun jamming. He had to believe they met for a reason. One he couldn't ignore. As though it were fated that they take this journey and find a way to build upon it.

He opened the file that Rosamund sent on Arnold Nishimoto, the creep Griswold hired to finish the job he started. It was pretty much as she had laid out. Nishimoto was a successful killer for hire and authorities had been unable to bring him in, making him all the more a threat to Rosamund and others who wound up in his crosshairs.

Russell reached out to his brother, Scott, for a video chat. Momentarily, he appeared on the screen.

"Hey," Scott said.

"Hey." Russell jutted his chin. "Got a sec?"

"Yeah." His brother flashed him a worried look. "What's up?"

"I need a favor."

"Okay," Scott said. "How can I help?"

"I need whatever the Bureau has on Arnold Nishimoto," Russell told him.

"Hmm...the name does ring a bell." Scott gazed at him. "Who is he?"

"Nishimoto's a hired killer," he informed his brother. "I'll send you a file the USMS put together on him."

"All right," Scott said. "Why your interest in Nishimoto? Is someone there being targeted by him?"

"Yeah, I'm afraid so." Russell creased his brow as he described the situation with Rosamund and her predicament, knowing that he could trust Scott. He didn't leave out the fact that he was sweet on the special agent, even while still coming to grips with her true identity versus the one he first knew her as.

"Wow!" Scott's eyes widened. "Annette and Madison mentioned that you were seeing someone. Figured you'd get around to telling me sooner or later. But this puts your love life in an entirely different light."

"Tell me about it," Russell muttered, while thinking that anything worthwhile was worth fighting for. The way he saw it, Rosamund definitely fit into that category. "Needless to say, before I can see if there's legs to this relationship, I have to make sure Rosamund lives to testify against her partner's killer, Simon Griswold."

"I hear you," Scott said evenly. "I'll see what I

can dig up on Nishimoto and see if the Bureau's intel is any different than the USMS file on the killer."

"Thanks, Scott."

"Anytime," he insisted.

After Russell ended the conversation, there was a knock on the door and Gloria Choi came in. "So, what did you find out about the connection between Deputy Marshal Leah Redfield and Tisha González, who's being called a Good Samaritan around here for preventing a child abduction?"

Though Russell wanted to satisfy her curiosity, while eliminating anything that could place Tisha in a bad light with the detective where it concerned Redfield, he knew he wouldn't be able to reveal that Rosamund was in WITSEC. Not just yet. As a delicate situation where any leak to the wrong person in the department could put Rosamund in danger, Russell had to keep this to himself. He considered that someone in the department had leaked her alias to a writer, which in and of itself was a no-no that could have placed Tisha in peril. Not that he believed for one minute that Gloria was a threat to Rosamund in any way. Or unable to play by the rules of witness protection. But with Redfield's death under mysterious circumstances and a chance that Nishimoto may have been responsible and was in town gunning for Rosamund, it wasn't a good idea to put her at further risk by exposing her. If the chief chose to expand those in the know, he would deal with it then.

For now, Russell only wanted to manage the situation as best he could.

"Redfield and Tisha were acquaintances," he told the detective with a straight face. "They both liked to jog and did so together sometimes. Tisha was broken up over Redfield's death."

"I see." Gloria regarded him contemplatively. "Does she have any idea why Redfield would kill herself?"

Russell pondered the question, before answering candidly, "Tisha didn't see Redfield as suicidal. I'm not sure I do either."

"Hmm…then you're talking about a faked suicide," she said. "Or the murder of a deputy marshal?"

Knowing what he did, he said bluntly, "I think it's a distinct possibility."

"And one more headache for us to deal with," Gloria moaned. "Along with the feds who, if it turns out to be true, will undoubtedly want to take the lead on this investigation."

"I'm guessing they already have," Russell argued, knowing from his work with the Bureau that any deaths, no matter the circumstances, needed to be investigated from within the federal agency involved for their own satisfaction as to when, how, and why a death occurred.

ROSAMUND SAT ON the sofa with the laptop on her legs as she contacted Harold Paxton for a video chat. She wondered if, with Leah's death, he would want to move her. If so, what would that do to her chances of making things work with Russell? Could they come back from the distrust he may feel now regarding her motivations for becoming intimate with him? Could he not see that her actions in becoming close to him were as real as anything she had ever felt in her life? Or would convincing Russell that she was falling in love with him be an uphill battle? That was further complicated by her agreeing to testify against Simon Griswold, which had brought her to Weconta Falls and Russell in the first place.

When Paxton appeared on screen, he had a dour look on his face. "Hey," he started equably, "I just got off the phone with Monroe Cortez. He briefed me on the tragic death of Leah Redfield. I'm sorry you've had to deal with this, on top of everything else."

"Me too." Rosamund took a soft breath and thought about Russell having come into her life as a result of being put in witness protection. "I'm having a hard time believing that Leah took her own life," she told him frankly. "I fear that something more ominous than that may be at work here."

"I understand how you feel," Paxton indicated. "We're cooperating with the U.S. Marshals Service in doing everything possible to get to the bottom of it. But as things now stand, the sentiments are that this was a suicide caused by job stress and financial woes, as Redfield was apparently heavily in debt.

These things were overlooked when she was assigned to be your handler. Cortez has assured me that her replacement, Patrick McDermott, is rock solid and has an exemplary record with the USMS."

Rosamund felt somewhat relieved to hear this, but doubts about Leah's death still lingered. "What's the status on Arnold Nishimoto?"

Paxton rubbed his nose. "Still no sign of him. We have federal agents and marshals searching far and wide. He's likely onto us and may be in disguise, while seeking to elude capture. Hopefully, it won't be long before we get him, one way or the other."

Rosamund wasn't convinced that the hitman would be apprehended anytime soon. She sensed that he was bent on carrying out his assignment, based on previous successes as a hired killer. "Is it possible that Arnold Nishimoto got to Leah, in trying to get to me, making it seem like she committed suicide?"

"We have no indication that Nishimoto is in California," the special agent in charge asserted. "Much less, has discovered you're hidden away in Weconta Falls. Of course, if it's determined that Deputy Marshal Redfield was murdered, then that would change everything. We'd get you out of there in a hurry."

"Only to have Nishimoto follow me elsewhere," Rosamund surmised cynically, "determined to finish the job."

"That's not going to happen." Paxton frowned.

"We need you to stay strong. Your testimony is of utmost importance in Simon Griswold's trial, to make sure he pays for the murder of Johnnie Langford, attempting to murder you, along with the human trafficking charges. If you feel unsafe there, I'll make arrangements with the USMS to relocate you elsewhere as soon as possible. Just say the word."

I don't really want to leave here, Rosamund told herself. At least not before the trial, giving her the time to try to make things right between her and Russell. Assuming they still had a future to work toward. She hoped with all her heart that was the case. But first, she had to survive the nightmare of being pursued like an animal by an assassin. "I'll stick it out here till the trial, which should be as safe as the next place," she contended. "A police officer has been posted outside the townhouse. And I believe that other members of the Weconta Falls PD are looking out for me as well." Especially Russell. Rosamund was sure that, in spite of the recent strain on their relationship, he still cared about her.

"Good," Paxton said, cracking a grin. "You'll get through this, Agent Santiago."

Rosamund nodded, wanting to believe it, and then asked, "Any news on the mole within the organization?"

He shook his head. "Nothing I can share at the moment," he said. "I can assure you, though, that we're doing everything we can to expose the individual and hold them accountable."

"All right." She wondered what he might be holding back from her, if anything. The idea that whoever was responsible for setting up Johnnie to be murdered, and nearly costing her own life as well, riled Rosamund. She could only hope the DHS and HSI Dallas Field Office would get to the bottom of it and that there would be justice.

An hour later, Rosamund echoed the same sentiments over the phone to Russell, who called to check on her. "I'm sure they'll discover who the mole is," he said. "The federal law enforcement agencies are usually pretty good at this type of thing when dealing with the ultimate in betrayal."

"You're right," she said, knowing that traitors within the DHS would not be tolerated, with the success of future missions at stake. She was sitting on the sofa, legs curled beneath her, happy to hear his voice, even if the tension between them was still evident.

"I sent my brother the file on Arnold Nishimoto," Russell informed her. "If the Bureau has anything more on him that might help to track Nishimoto down, Scott will let me know."

"Thanks. It's no fun having a hired killer bent on taking you out," Rosamund voiced humorlessly.

"I know. I can only imagine how difficult it must

be to have to deal with this. But Nishimoto will fail," Russell insisted.

"I wonder how many of his other victims were told the same thing," she questioned, "before he finished them off?"

"That's a fair point." He sighed. "Now that I know what's going on, I'll do everything in my power to ensure your safety while you're in Weconta Falls. Even beyond. The chief is backing me on this. That includes the presence of Officer Kevin Wilkinson outside your door, over and beyond the arrival of your new handler, and greater coordination with the U.S. Marshals Service. I'll also be available whenever you need me. If Nishimoto is somehow able to learn your location and foolish enough to show his face in town, we'll be ready for him."

"Thank you." Rosamund felt better about the situation, even though she was still concerned that Leah's death may not have been self-inflicted. She considered that the deputy marshal could have been targeted by someone other than Arnold Nishimoto, for whatever reason.

"Just doing my job," Russell suggested. Abruptly, he changed course, admitting, "It's more than a job. Whether you're Tisha González or Rosamund Santiago, I still care about you and want to see where we can go with this. Assuming you feel the same way, now that your cards have been laid out on the table and I know who you are and why you're here."

"I do feel the same way, Russell," she made clear. "I just think we need to dial things back a bit till we see how this plays out with the trial and what comes after." It pained her to have to say that, especially knowing the way she felt about him, but Rosamund didn't want to set up any false expectations for either of them. Russell deserved to be with someone who could fit into the life he'd made for himself in Weconta Falls. Whether with her or another woman. She just wasn't sure if that could be her with the life she had established elsewhere.

"I agree," he told her without prelude. "You're under enough pressure as it is without my adding to it by making demands on your time or expectations for the future. Let's concentrate on keeping you alive for now. Anything else will work itself out."

"Okay." Rosamund felt relieved that he was so understanding. And at the same time, was willing to keep the door open for a future that she hoped to still have with him. Wherever that might take them. She said good-night, while wondering if she would actually be able to sleep at all, given the twists and turns the day had taken.

ARNOLD NISHIMOTO SAT in a wide barrel chair in a cheap motel room on the edge of town. He was holding an iPad Air and reading an article on the webpage of the *Weconta Falls Journal*. It was written by Freddie Hildebrand, who talked about a Good

Samaritan waitress named Tisha González, who singlehandedly took down a would-be child abductor, Paul Skinner. The brazen risk to her own life to save another was admirable to Nishimoto. He hated creeps who went after children and hoped Skinner rotted away in prison. Unfortunately, that act of courage wasn't enough to save Tisha González, otherwise known as Rosamund Santiago, special agent for Homeland Security Investigations. Moreover, she was the fed's star witness in a case against Simon Griswold and, as such, needed to be eliminated.

That was just what Nishimoto planned to do to Rosamund Santiago, put her out to pasture permanently, as he was paid to do. Now that he knew where she worked and lived, the rest would be a mere formality. "Gotcha now, Tisha," he said out loud, and then laughed at the thought.

He skimmed more of the article, then set the iPad on a wooden table and grabbed a can of beer. Drinking a generous amount, Nishimoto thought about the deputy marshal who had served as the special agent's handler. He had managed to track her down and forced her to drive to a construction zone where the crew had gone home for the day. Using Redfield's own gun, he had shot her to death and made it look like a suicide, bolstered by the fentanyl he had given her.

Soon, Nishimoto planned to make quick work in disposing of Rosamund Santiago. Then he could make his exit from Weconta Falls as effortlessly as he had arrived in town. *Enjoy the short time you have left, Tisha González,* Nishimoto told himself, as he finished off the beer.

Chapter Eleven

The next morning, Rosamund was already dressed for her shift at the restaurant later in the day when she welcomed inside the townhouse Deputy U.S. Marshal Patrick McDermott. Before entering, he had to be cleared by Officer Wilkinson, a forty-year-old, thickly built and sandy-haired family man, who Rosamund learned had three kids and two dogs, to enter. Still, McDermott flashed his identification all the same, so she felt comfortable in having him as her new handler. He was tall with a solid build, and he wore a navy suit and cap toe, lace-up black shoes.

"Sorry to have to be here under these circumstances," he remarked lamentably. "Deputy Marshal Redfield was a great member of the team, a friend, and a good person."

"Yes, she was," Rosamund agreed, from what little she knew of her. "I too am sorry for what happened to her." She paused, realizing this was as awkward for him as it was for her. Not only was she outside her comfort zone, having been temporarily relocated from her normal habitat, but just as she was starting to form a rapport with Leah, the handler was gone. Had she really taken her own life? "Would you like a cup of coffee?" Rosamund asked the deputy marshal.

"Sure, I'd love one," McDermott told her.

"Same here." She smiled at him, wondering if he would last as her handler. Or would she end up being sent packing again and need a new handler to work with? After making the two cups of coffee and adding cream and sugar to McDermott's cup at his request, Rosamund handed it to him and they sat in the dining room. "So, how did you end up becoming a U.S. marshal?" she asked casually.

"To make a long story short," he said, "I started off being a deputy recruiting officer and worked my way into a full-time job as a deputy U.S. marshal. I wanted to play a larger role in the U.S. Marshals Service, be it protecting witnesses, such as yourself, or dealing with prisoners, or tracking down fugitives." He sipped the coffee. "I've read your file."

"Hope you weren't too bored," she quipped, tasting the coffee.

"Quite the opposite." He grinned momentarily, then became serious. "Sorry to hear about your partner, Johnnie Langford. Seems like as HSI special agents, together you played a big role in breaking up human and sex trafficking rings in Texas."

"We did the best we could," Rosamund said modestly, while thinking about the very high price

Johnnie paid in trying to do his part in the process. "Honestly, sometimes it feels like an uphill battle."

"But usually worth it in the end, right?"

"Yes, I suppose." She sipped more coffee pensively.

"I'm sure you're eager to get past being in the Witness Security Program," McDermott stated, "so you can get on with your life?"

Rosamund offered a weak smile in response, knowing there were mixed feelings on that score. She definitely was keen on putting WITSEC behind her, but wasn't nearly as eager to have to leave what she had started with Russell behind. How could she ever return to a life that was void of romance and the person who could be in her corner away from the job? "So, how will this work as my new handler?" she asked, knowing that he wasn't a local and likely wasn't expected to shadow her 24/7, so long as a viable and immediate threat to her safety had not been firmly established as a witness in protection.

"I'll be renting a place nearby," McDermott explained. "You'll have my number and I'll be in regular communication with you. I'll also work closely with the Weconta Falls Police Department should trouble arise, with Police Chief Diane O'Shea entirely cooperative. And Detective Russell Lynley being made available as additional backup, in case he's needed to keep you safe or thwart an attack."

"Sounds good." Rosamund resisted a smile as she

thought of Russell going from a detective she was dating to someone offering protection to her from a hitman. In both instances, she felt fortunate to have Russell play a bigger role in her life, on and off the job. Even if it could only be short-lived, once she was no longer in the program.

After McDermott left in a metallic silver Lincoln Corsair Reserve, Rosamund notified the officer on duty that she was headed to work, knowing he would follow and make sure no one else was following. She wondered if Russell would stop by for coffee or lunch. Or had the routine taken a hit, now that he knew waitressing was not her primary occupation but just a stopgap measure till she could reestablish her occupation in law enforcement.

"THE SERIAL NUMBER of the Glock 27 pistol that was used to kill Deputy U.S. Marshal Leah Redfield was confirmed to be Redfield's official firearm as a member of the USMS," Ike Wainright told Russell, after Ike had come from the Weconta Falls PD Crime Lab.

Russell wasn't particularly surprised with this forensic finding, considering where the weapon was found relative to the cause of death. Still, he had to ask, "And what about the slug removed from Redfield's head?"

Ike creased his brow. "Forensics found it to be a match for the shell casing found on the floor of Redfield's vehicle," he said. "The bullet itself was

a match for a test fired bullet from the deputy marshal's gun and both bullets came through the same
gun's barrel with a left-hand twist and four lands and
grooves. In other words, Redfield was killed with her
own weapon and, based on the trajectory and proximity, it still appears to have been self-inflicted."

"Maybe," Russell muttered, knowing that appear-
ances could be deceiving. Especially if someone had
good reason to deceive them. Such as Arnold Nishimoto, in spite of having no evidence that he was in
town and had been able to take out the experienced
deputy marshal as a means to more easily be able
to go after Rosamund. "We need to check out the
surveillance footage in the area where Redfield's
car was found. I know that warehouse was under
construction, meaning there likely wasn't a security system in place yet. But other cameras may be
able to tell us if any other cars came or left around
the same time. Or, for that matter, may even show if
anyone was in the vehicle with the deputy marshal
at the time she supposedly shot herself to death."

"Worth a try," Ike agreed. "Maybe a long shot, but
if Redfield didn't kill herself, someone sure wants us
to believe that and, thereby, to get away with murder."

Russell nodded. "Let's see what we come up with."
He went into his office and found a preliminary toxicology report on Leah Redfield on his desk. As he
read it, he saw that the deputy U.S. marshal had a

high concentration of fentanyl in her system. The report implied that it may have been contributory to her death. This was troubling to him, as random drug testing administered to federal employees would have likely detected drug use if she had been using fentanyl prior to this, not to mention abusing it. As such, Russell had to wonder if the drug had been given to Redfield against her will, as a prelude to murdering her.

This brought him back to the notion that Redfield could have been targeted. Russell admitted that it would take some getting used to for him to refer to Tisha now as Rosamund, her real name. But he was prepared to do that, if it meant separating the waitress from an HSI special agent whose testimony would help bring down a human trafficking ring. As for their personal relationship, he was also up to allowing that to play out, hopefully for the better.

His cell phone buzzed and Russell removed it from the back pocket of his trousers. The caller was from his brother, Scott. After sitting at his desk, Russell connected with him. "Hey."

"Got some news on Arnold Nishimoto," Scott said.

"Okay." Russell adjusted in the seat with expectation.

"Did some digging around and learned that, apart from his given name, Nishimoto is also known to use two aliases in evading authorities. Aaron Kamekona and Lyle Satoshige. I'm guessing he could be using any of the three right now, including multiple passports and fake IDs to that effect."

"Hmm…" Russell made a mental note of this new development. "Send me those names," he requested. "I'll see if any of them show up with any rental car companies between here and San Francisco, local hotels and motels, and the like."

"You think Nishimoto is in Weconta Falls?"

"Not necessarily," Russell responded. "That would mean he was able to break through the U.S. Marshals Service barriers in safeguarding the new identity and location of witnesses." He drew a breath. "On the other hand, as a paid and ruthless assassin, Nishimoto will likely do whatever it takes to locate his target and complete the mission. As such, we can't afford to minimize the risk he poses to Rosamund's safety."

"I can see you really care for her," Scott told him.

"Yeah, I do," he responded without preamble. More than he had cared for anyone since losing Victoria. He didn't take that lightly, no matter how he and Rosamund got to this point. "Beyond that, I care about law and order and keeping all residents of Weconta Falls, even temporary ones, safe from known enemies and real threats."

"I hear you," his brother said. "Whatever more I can do to help, let me know."

"I will, Scott, and thanks," Russell said sincerely.

"Anytime."

"Later." After ending the call, Russell got back on his feet to head over to Shailene's Grill, where he knew Rosamund was back at work as her waitressing alter ego, Tisha.

"ARE YOU READY to order?" Rosamund asked the thirtysomething, bald-headed Asian man, who wore cat-eye glasses.

He gave her a soft grin. "Yes," he said. "I'll go with the green tea and avocado toast."

"Sounds good." She smiled at him. "Coming right up."

"Thanks." He met her eyes briefly, then turned to his cell phone that seemed to have some messages.

Rosamund put in the order and then went to wait on other patrons of Shailene's Grill. She admittedly felt a little weird still operating as Tisha González, now that the truth about who she was had been revealed. At least to Russell. She wondered if he would treat her differently now. Would their romantic involvement survive? Or would this new reality be too much of a hurdle to overcome for both of them? *I'll just have to see where it goes with us*, Rosamund told herself, as she delivered the order of avocado toast and green tea to the gentleman, who seemed grateful, as if she had done something special.

When the bell over the door rang to indicate someone new had entered, Rosamund turned to look, hoping it was Russell. She felt disappointed when she saw that instead it was a group of loud teenagers, recognizing them as the ones who had accosted her at the park. They sat around a table and the female glanced her way, but didn't seem to recognize her. Rosamund watched as Tracy went to take their orders. *I hope they haven't harassed anyone else in the park*, Rosamund thought, unsure just how much Russell had left an impression on them about going down the wrong path. She commended him nevertheless for feeling they were worth trying to reform before it was too late. It was yet another reason why she had fallen for the man and didn't want to lose what they had. She hoped he felt the same way at the end of the day.

When the bell over the door rang a few minutes later, Rosamund's eyes lit up when she saw that, this time, it was Russell. She eagerly headed his way, even as she felt butterflies in her stomach for what could be on his mind.

RUSSELL'S HEART SKIPPED a beat as he laid eyes on Rosamund, still looking great as a waitress, but with what looked to be a new level of confidence with his knowledge of her real occupation that rivaled his days with the FBI. If not more impressive and certainly just as important in the continuous fight against criminality. He took the last remaining table near the window, which wasn't his usual one. He barely noticed the Asian man leaving the restaurant, but did home in on the teens, remembering them from their run-in with Rosamund at Weconta Falls Park. He wondered if she noticed them. How could she not, given they were making noise, looking for attention. When they saw him, the group toned down the sounds, not willing to try his patience. Fortunately, for the most part, they seemed to have limited their misbehavior of late to normal teenage pranks and otherwise harmless activities.

"Hey," Rosamund came up to him, offering a nice smile, as if it was just another day of flirtations between them. He was game in doing his part in maintaining the facade, while believing in his heart that much of what existed between them was real.

"Hey," he told her. "Can we talk?"

"Sure. Give me five minutes to get someone to cover for me."

"All right." He watched her walk away and Russell found himself amazed at just how well Rosamund, as Tisha, had managed to fit in at Shailene's Grill. Though he knew some people who had been successfully placed in WITSEC, he had never been able to put himself in their shoes. Till now. Or at least somewhat in picturing everything Rosamund had given up in entering the program, including the loss of her HSI partner. Could she reenter her real life without missing a beat, while leaving the short-term life established in Weconta Falls behind? Including the bond they had formed?

Russell realized that his own relocation to the town had not been so different. He had turned his back on the life he had before, albeit with more of a choice in the matter, unable to cope fully with losing his wife and daughter. Could he go back, leaving behind the new relationships he had forged in Weconta Falls with his colleagues and some friends?

"Coffee, black," Rosamund said, interrupting his musings.

"Thanks." He grinned crookedly, as she sat across from him. "Has everything gone all right for you today?" He needed to know.

"Yes, thus far." She studied him. "Did you have reason to believe otherwise?"

Russell tasted the steaming coffee. "We were able to confirm that Leah Redfield was killed with her own weapon," he reported in a low voice. "And the preliminary toxicology report indicates that she had a high level of fentanyl in her body at the time of death."

Rosamund frowned. "Leah couldn't have been a drug addict," she whispered confidently.

"I tend to agree with you there. Yet the fentanyl was in her system, leaving me to believe, when combined with the alleged suicide, the deputy marshal's death may have been staged."

"By whom?" She locked eyes with him. "You think Arnold Nishimoto could be behind Leah's death?"

Russell sipped more coffee. He hated to go down this road, but there was no sugarcoating his concern that the very assassin who had forced her to go into hiding could well have found her. "I learned from the FBI that Nishimoto has two aliases they know of that he uses, leaving me to believe it's at least possible that he has learned of your location and killed your handler in the process of trying to gather more information on your identity and whereabouts."

Rosamund put a trembling hand to her mouth. "Nishimoto here...in Weconta Falls?"

Russell reached out and touched her hand comfortingly. "There's been no positive confirmation of that yet," he stressed. "The odds are still in your favor that Nishimoto is completely in the dark as to your whereabouts and that Leah Redfield could well have taken her own life and been abusing fentanyl surreptitiously. We're checking to see if Nishimoto has accessed anything locally, such as accommodations, under his own name or one of his fake monikers. He may also have changed his appearance. Have you noticed anyone in here asking questions or otherwise acting suspicious?"

"Not really," she said contemplatively, "if I don't count the teenagers over there from the park. But they are who they are and, apparently, proud of it." Rosamund wrinkled her nose.

"I think they learned their lesson," Russell contended, though not in any way seeking to justify their delinquent behavior.

"There was this one guy..." She turned her head to a table that was now empty.

"What about him?" Russell asked curiously.

"Well, there was nothing in particular," she muttered, "except that I hadn't seen him in here before."

"What did he look like?"

She described an Asian male in his thirties and bald-headed, wearing glasses. "I suppose that could have been Arnold Nishimoto," she speculated. "Or just an innocent man who happened in here for green tea and avocado toast."

"Hmm..." Russell sipped his coffee, lost in thought. Could Nishimoto have been brazen enough to hide in plain view in order to check out his target in advance of the kill? "Maybe security video will show him and how he got here."

Her lashes fluttered. "And if that was Nishimoto?"

"Then he's even more dangerous than ever." Russell pulled no punches in this regard. "Either way, if it's all the same to you, I seriously think you should move into my house for now. There's plenty of room. I can clear it with your handler and the DHS, but it's more isolated, secure, and less desirable a place for Nishimoto to go after you."

"Yes, of course, I'll stay with you," Rosamund gave in meekly. "Better safe than sorry, right?"

"Absolutely," he concurred. "I'll arrange for Offi-

cer Wilkinson to accompany you back to the townhouse to pick up some things, make sure you aren't
being followed, and bring you to my place." He took
out his house key and handed it to her. "I keep a
spare in my car. With any luck, it'll all turn out to
be a false alarm and you can carry on with your life
here for as long as you need to." Which, in his mind,
would be long enough for them to continue to build
a solid rapport that could force them to make some
hard choices when the time was right.

"Okay." Rosamund stood up. "Have to get back
to my day job," she quipped, showing she still had
a sense of humor, even in the midst of danger and
uncertainty.

"I better do the same," Russell told her, finishing
off the coffee and rising. He grinned. "Thanks for the
chat, Tisha."

She made a face playfully and walked away. He
would send someone later to check out the surveillance video from the restaurant, so as not to risk
blowing Rosamund's cover, just yet.

Outside, Russell scanned the area, wondering if
the suspect might still be lurking around. He saw no
one. He glanced across the street at the apartment
building, noting people coming and going normally,
but no sign of someone fitting the description of the
man. *Maybe I'm grasping at straws here*, Russell
told himself. Or maybe Tisha's customer truly was
Arnold Nishimoto in disguise.

Russell conferred briefly with Officer Kevin Wilkinson. He was seated in his squad car outside the restaurant, but close enough to act if Rosamund gave him the prearranged sign to say she was in trouble. After making sure they were on the same page, Russell headed back to the department, having a whole new reason for returning to his FBI roots as a small-town detective, trying to keep a special lady safe from a deadly hunter.

ARNOLD NISHIMOTO WAS pleased with himself for being right under the dainty little nose of his next target, Homeland Security Investigations Special Agent Rosamund Santiago, as she masqueraded as small-town waitress Tisha González. If only she had a clue that the mild-mannered man she was serving green tea and avocado toast was really far more interested in sizing her up for what would be her last full day on earth. She foolishly believed she was safe and sound in Weconta Falls, out of his reach under the protection of the U.S. Marshals Service and local police department. It was this overconfidence and lack of appreciation of his skills and determination that would lead to the special agent's untimely demise.

Only then could he collect on the balance of the substantial payment Simon Griswold was willing to dole out to see Rosamund Santiago dead. Climbing behind the wheel of his latest rental car, a blue Mitsubishi Outlander Sport SE, Nishimoto cracked a devious smile as the perfect plan of action started to take shape in his mind. The special agent would never see it coming before her life ended. By the time her protectors tried to come to her aide, they would be left scratching their collective heads as she paid the ultimate price for getting on the wrong side of the human trafficker Griswold.

As he drove off and past Shailene's Grill, Nishimoto grinned again and muttered satisfyingly, "See you soon, Agent Santiago. Very soon."

Chapter Twelve

When he arrived home, Russell gave Officer Wilkinson the rest of the evening off. Unsure how awkward it might be having Rosamund there in a whole new light, Russell was surprised when he stepped inside and heard music. She was playing a Frank Sinatra album on the turntable. Even more surprising was that Rosamund had made them dinner and seemed perfectly relaxed. "If I'm going to possibly be here for a while, I figured I may as well contribute," she explained. "Starting with some good music and learning my way around the kitchen. I combined some of your leftovers with ingredients I picked up at the supermarket for homemade chicken stew and cranberry bread."

"Great choice in music." He grinned appreciatively. "As for the food, it smells delicious, Rosamund," he said, beginning to feel at ease referring to her by her real name.

"Hopefully, that will be matched by the taste," she teased with a chuckle.

"I'm sure it will be." Frankly, nothing surprised Russell anymore about the special agent who seemed more than capable of doing anything she set her mind to. Minutes later, he had washed up and they were seated at the dining room table, eating. "It's good," he told her, as expected, after tasting the chicken stew.

Rosamund blushed. "I just want to carry my own weight while I'm sharing this space with you."

"Your weight is perfect for your size," Russell couldn't help but say. It was but one of her many qualities that captured his fancy. He smiled. "But I'm sure you already know that."

"I do what I need to for maintaining a proper weight and staying in shape," she said coolly. "Which obviously applies to you as well."

"I try," he said, flattered, and bit off a chunk of cranberry bread.

"Any more news on Arnold Nishimoto?" Rosamund looked worried as she lifted a spoonful of chicken stew to her mouth.

"Nothing yet." Russell wished he could say differently. "No indication that Nishimoto is in Weconta Falls. We're still studying surveillance videos and using face recognition software to try to determine if he's anywhere in the vicinity."

"Good luck with that." She wrinkled her nose. "The man's made a career out of eluding the authorities. No telling what he's got up his sleeve to try to silence me. Including possibly taking out Leah as a warning sign."

Russell didn't disagree with her, as far as the hired killer's capabilities. But he wasn't about to allow Rosamund to believe it was hopeless to stop Nishimoto from ultimately carrying out the hit. "Redfield's death may or may not be a matter of foul play," he stated, using a napkin to wipe the corner of his mouth. "That's yet to be determined, notwithstanding the medical examiner making it a probable suicide. Either way, between the USMS, DHS, and the Weconta Falls PD, myself included, we'll make sure nothing stops you from testifying at Simon Griswold's trial."

"Okay." Rosamund sighed. "I'll just be glad when it's over."

"It will be, soon enough," Russell told her. "I promise." He wondered if being over meant them too. The notion that she would simply walk out of his life for good didn't sit well with him. He lifted a glass of water and took a sip, figuring this might be a good time to address a related issue on his mind in an attempt to get to know more about the real her. "So, I get that you needed a new identity and back story while in WITSEC, but was there at least a grain of truth about your family dynamics?"

"Actually, more than a grain." She shifted in the side chair uncomfortably while meeting his eyes. "My parents really are semiretired in Florida," she said candidly. "They moved to the Keys from Texas a few years ago and seem to be happy. My younger sister, Gabby, is married to an allergist and has two children, Zach and Nina. Only they live in Ohio instead of Nebraska."

"I see." He was glad to know she wasn't too far off about the family she was forced to be apart from. "Any real relation to Cranston, Rhode Island?" he asked curiously.

"My college roommate is from Cranston," Rosamund responded. "I spent spring break there with her once and it was the first place I could think of when asked to choose a new location that I was from. I figured it was unlikely that Griswold or his hired killer would ever make the connection."

Russell smiled. "I think you're right about that."

She smiled back and he remembered that it was one of her qualities that attracted him. And the list went on. He could only hope that what drew them together didn't somehow end up pulling them apart.

ROSAMUND KNEW SHE had a good thing—make that great thing—with Russell Lynley. She didn't want to throw that away, no matter how things turned out with the trial and afterward. Didn't she and Russell owe it to themselves to see if they could get beyond their separate lives and work toward a life that could bring them together? She felt heartened by his offer to put her up while a hired assassin remained at large and possibly aware of her location and new identity. Apart from the fact that Russell had gone over and beyond the call of duty as a Weconta Falls detective, Rosamund sensed that his feelings for her had not changed, in spite of having to adjust to her being someone other than waitress Tisha González. Just as she felt the same for him as before. He was someone who tugged at her heartstrings in ways she had never experienced before.

When they slow danced in his living room to the mellow voice of Tony Bennett, Rosamund gave in to her desire to want to be with Russell, pushing aside any reservations that what they had wasn't real. They ended up in his bedroom, where they comforted each other through the night. Their lovemaking was all-consuming, energetic, and just what she needed to occupy her thoughts, instead of the nagging fears that Arnold Nishimoto had the jump on her and would soon make his presence felt.

IN THE MORNING, Russell quietly slipped from Rosamund's grasp. If it were up to him, he'd stay in bed with her around the clock. She had come to mean that much to him. So much so that he may have let it slip out during sex that he loved her. Or maybe the words were in his head, but no less true. They had time to sort out what that meant and where she stood later. Right now, he needed to stay on top of the law enforcement efforts to keep Rosamund protected from the contract killer.

Russell thought Rosamund looked like a beautiful angel while asleep in his bed. He hoped this could last forever, but would gladly take one day at a time. He got dressed and, in the living room, called Officer Wilkinson to resume his official guard duty of Rosamund. Then Russell called Deputy Marshal Patrick McDermott to update him.

"I'll swing by Shailene's Grill when Rosamund goes to work," McDermott said, "and spell Officer Wilkinson. If anything seems out of sorts, I'll get the cavalry there, pronto."

"Sounds good," Russell told him. "Heard anything on the investigation by the USMS into the death of Leah Redfield?" It had now become a joint operation to look into the suspicious passing of one of their own, with suicide seeming less and less likely, given the red flags that made it questionable in the minds of some, himself included. Particularly the threat that Redfield posed as Rosamund's handler to an assassin fixated on making sure Rosamund didn't live long enough to testify against Simon Griswold.

"Only that a memorial service will be held for Leah this weekend in her hometown of Citrus Heights, California," the deputy marshal announced. "As for her death, no one who knew her believes she would end it all like that. Not when she had so much to live for."

Russell lowered his chin. "I was thinking the same thing." The trick now was to prove their case, while at the same time confronting whoever might have killed Redfield. And temporarily, at least, left Rosamund vulnerable to attack.

THE SURVEILLANCE FOOTAGE of what appeared to be Leah Redfield's red Buick Encore was taken from a nearby building as the deputy marshal drove to-ward the spot on Breckton Street where her vehi-cle was found, close to the estimated time of death. "That definitely looks like Redfield's car," Russell remarked, sitting before the laptop on his desk, with Gloria hovering over his shoulder.

"It does," she agreed. "Home in on the license plate."

He did just that and, as expected, they were able to quickly establish that it was indeed Deputy Marshal Redfield's official vehicle with the USMS. "There appears to be two occupants in the car," Russell noted. He zoomed in on the still image, studying it.

"Redfield's the driver," Gloria ascertained. "The individual in the passenger seat is male. Can you get a better shot of him?"

"Yeah, I think so." Russell brought the image closer. Though somewhat grainy, it still gave a rea-sonable picture of a bald man who looked to be in his thirties and could have been Asian.

"Does he look familiar?" Gloria asked.

Russell immediately thought of the person who Rosamund had described from Shailene's Grill. The car occupant fit the description. But he didn't exactly look like the photo of Arnold Nishimoto in the file of the wanted hitman. Had he changed his appearance?

"Maybe," Russell said vaguely. Not willing to tip his hand quite yet. "If this guy murdered Redfield and fled the scene of the crime, he obviously didn't leave in her car. So how did he get away?"

"In another vehicle?" Gloria deduced. "Maybe he forced Redfield to that location, having already determined there were no security cameras in a new construction zone, killed her with her own gun, and made his escape."

It made sense to Russell, considering the circumstances and Redfield found shot to death, with no one else in sight. "Let's see what cars passed in the opposite direction shortly after Redfield's vehicle drove by." He fast-forwarded the video footage till he saw a single car driving by, less than five minutes after Redfield had driven in the opposite direction.

Gloria asked, her voice lifted an octave, "You think that could be him?"

"Let's have a look." Russell rewound to get a closer look at the vehicle and driver. It was a dark blue Mitsubishi Outlander Sport SE. Zooming in on the driver, it was almost certainly the same man who had been in Redfield's car. "I think we may be on to something," he told her.

"I think you're right," she agreed. "Home in on the vehicle's license plate and we'll see who the car belongs to." After Russell did that, Gloria took down the info and said, "Back in a sec."

After she left the office, Russell pulled up the surveillance video he requested showing the parking lot at Shailene's Grill yesterday. He was able to find footage of a man who fit the description Rosamund gave of the Asian customer, leaving the restaurant in the right time frame. Comparing the image with that of the man seen driving with Deputy Marshal Redfield and the man driving a different vehicle alone, it seemed like a match to Russell. Could this be Arnold Nishimoto, hidden in plain view?

Opening the file on Nishimoto, Russell looked at his photograph and compared it with the others. It appeared to be the same man. But what if he was wrong? He accessed the facial recognition software the Weconta Falls Police Department used, along with the Departments of Justice and Homeland Security, to help identify and track down known and unknown offenders. After supplying information, it came up with an apparent hit to indicate a strong probability that Arnold Nishimoto was the suspect in question and likely had murdered Leah Redfield to get at Rosamund.

Gloria came back into the office and said, an edge to her tone, "Turns out the car is registered to a rental car company in Oakland, California. It was rented to a man named Lyle Satoshige."

"Lyle Satoshige is an alias for reputed hitman Arnold Nishimoto," Russell stated with a sinking feeling in the pit of his stomach.

Gloria hoisted a brow. "Why would this Nishimoto kill the deputy marshal?"

After sucking in a deep breath, Russell looked her in the eye and said, "Because she was standing in the way of his real target, Homeland Security Investigations Special Agent Rosamund Santiago." Russell knew it was time to let the detective in on the situation, sure that Diane O'Shea would agree, given the gravity of where things stood. "You know her as the Good Samaritan waitress, Tisha González."

As Gloria's mouth dropped open in stunned silence, Russell filled her in on the need-to-know basis details of Rosamund's protection under the U.S. Witness Security Program and planned testimony against Simon Griswold. Afterward, Russell turned his attention and sense of urgency to determining Nishimoto's base of operations, sensing that every second counted in preventing him from carrying out his mission.

As usual for Rosamund, there was a steady stream of hungry and thirsty customers in the morning rush at Shailene's Grill. Even Shailene McEnany herself, the co-owner, was in on the action, filling in where she was needed. In this case, it was as a waitress, substituting for Tracy, who had to take one of her children to see the doctor for an ear infection. "Hope you don't abandon me too, Tisha," Shailene whined, half seriously, as they crossed paths with dueling plates of steaming stacks of buttermilk pancakes.

Rosamund had to remember her moniker, seeing that she had gone back to her real name partly, now that Russell was privy to it and slipped up himself a time or two. She wondered how long it would be before she was able to return to who she was full-time. Or was that even possible at this point? Especially when her heart belonged in Weconta Falls, so long as Russell remained there. "Wouldn't dream of it," she told Shailene with a straight face, knowing full well it was a promise she couldn't keep. But she still needed to play the part and stick with it for as long as was needed in the scheme of things.

"Good to hear." Shailene looked relieved. "Now why don't we deliver these hotcakes before they're no longer hot."

"Right." Rosamund chuckled. She took the order to the table and was about to go to another, when her cell phone chimed. She slipped it out of the front pocket of her uniform and saw a text message from Deputy Marshal Patrick McDermott that chilled her:

Detective Lynley has informed me that Arnold Nishimoto is the man you saw yesterday at restaurant. Could even be inside right now. Stay alert, but don't tip your hand. I'm on my way in.

Nishimoto found me? Rosamund thought in near panic, after wanting to believe she had safely evaded the hired killer by moving to Weconta Falls. She couldn't understand how this could have happened. She wondered if the mole within the DHS or HSI was responsible for passing along her whereabouts to Arnold Nishimoto.

Rosamund gulped as her eyes darted around furtively in search of the hitman, who had shaved his head to disguise his appearance and deadly intentions. She did not see him at first glance or even second, which concerned as much as relieved her. Had she missed him? Was he in disguise? Was it his plan to try to kill her in a crowded restaurant? She doubted that a skilled assassin would put himself in such a position to be identified and possibly tripped up before making an escape. No, he was biding his time. Waiting for the right moment to finish her off. But when exactly was that?

As she assessed the situation and imminent danger, Rosamund's first instincts were to reach for the Sig Sauer pistol she had taken recently to keeping in her ankle holster, while hoping to never have to use it. Especially in a packed restaurant. But she needed to keep a cool head and not make any sudden moves that could give Nishimoto the upper hand. Assuming he didn't already have it.

"Get a move on, Tisha!" Shailene yelled at her. "The food won't serve itself!"

"All right." Rosamund did as she was told, preferring the stress and strain of waitressing to dodging a tenacious hitman. She went about her job for now, while waiting for Deputy Marshal McDermott's instructions on how to proceed.

Chapter Thirteen

Russell was wearing a ballistic vest and holding his firearm, as he and other armed members of the Weconta Falls PD converged upon the Weconta Falls Motel, Room 157, on Yerdlyn Road, on the outskirts of town. It was where Arnold Nishimoto was believed to be staying, using the name Lyle Satoshige. The U.S. Marshals Service and Department of Homeland Security were notified of what Russell believed was a strong indication that the assassin they were looking for was in Weconta Falls.

In spite of no sign of Nishimoto's rented Mitsubishi Outlander, they weren't taking any chances that he could still be inside the room. Short of that, they needed to know if he left any clues of what he was up to. Russell gave the nod and the door to the room was unlocked with a key supplied by the manager of the motel. Storming inside, they found it was unoccupied, with the bed unmade and a half-eaten pizza left on a wooden table, along with an empty can of beer. With no clothes or luggage present, it was clear the hitman had no plans of returning. This was troubling to Russell, telling him that Nishimoto was very likely in the process of executing his plans to go after Rosamund.

"He left something," Ike said, having been apprised of the situation by the chief and Russell.

"What do you have there?" Russell asked, noting that Ike had pulled something out of the wastebasket.

"Looks like a diagram of an apartment building," he replied.

Russell put his gun away and looked at it. He recognized it as the five-story building directly across the street from Shailene's Grill. Why would that be of interest to Nishimoto? Then it hit Russell. The hitman intended to use it as a staging area to launch a deadly attack on Rosamund. *I have to warn her,* Russell told himself, his heart racing at the thought of Nishimoto gunning her down.

"It's an apartment building on Liverwood Street," Russell told Ike. "Shailene's Grill, where Rosamund is working as a waitress, is on the other side of the street. Nishimoto is planning to assassinate her there."

Ike frowned. "I'll get all available units to the area and we'll stop him from succeeding in his plan."

Russell nodded and said, "I'm heading over there." He then instructed Ike to update the DHS and USMS on the situation, before Russell raced to his car. Inside, he phoned McDermott, counting on him to protect Rosamund, as was his job. Though she was armed, Russell knew she was at a disadvantage in her current role, with her would-be killer having no such restraints.

In the end, Russell believed it was up to him to stop Nishimoto from succeeding with the hit, while hoping it wasn't already too late.

ARNOLD NISHIMOTO SCALED the stairs to the roof of the apartment building. He walked onto the roof and made his way to the front of the building and crouched low to avoid detection. He gazed across the street at Shailene's Grill. The place itself had floor-to-ceiling windows that were perfect for what he had planned for the fed's witness against Simon Griswold.

Nishimoto stepped away from the ledge and un-zipped his fabric rifle case. He removed the parts of a Nosler M21 rifle and began to assemble it. Once done, he took a haphazard 360-degree peek through the scope, before moving back to the ledge. Positioning himself, he took aim at the windows of the restaurant, knowing that at any moment Rosamund Santiago would be serving a customer sitting by the window. It was then that Nishimoto would finish her off and report to his client, Simon Griswold, that the work was done and it was time to be paid in full.

Show your pretty face, Rosamund, and this will be over, the hitman mused, feeling antsy for some reason, as though there was reason to be concerned that his target might somehow slip away from him.

"CHANGE OF PLANS," McDermott told Rosamund, as he ushered her to a corner, away from others. "We have reason to believe that Nishimoto is somewhere in the apartment building across the street, likely armed with a high-powered rifle, with plans to open fire at any time."

Feeling the heat of the moment, she assessed this frightening news and gazed at the deputy marshal. "Can you stop him?" She hated to think that Nishimoto could somehow escape and be free to go after other targets in the future.

"We're certainly going to try." McDermott spoke in earnest. "But in the meantime, we need to protect you. Is there a back exit?"

"Yes, but I can't just leave like that," Rosamund protested. "We're super busy and already short staffed as it is."

His brow furrowed. "I understand your concern here, but that's not really your problem," he argued. "It's staying alive till you're called upon to testify in a major human trafficking case. My job is to make sure you survive an attempt to keep you from testifying. We need to get you out of here, Special Agent Santiago." His voice dropped an octave. "I'm afraid this isn't up for debate."

Rosamund knew he was right and she had to comply. As much as she felt loyal to Shailene and had bonded with Tracy, her first and foremost obligation was to herself and the DHS's Center for Counter-

ing Human Trafficking. She owed it to the memory
of her late partner, Johnnie Langford, not to lose
sight of why she was waitressing at the restaurant,
instead of doing her real job fighting human smuggling, sexual exploitation of women and children,
and the like. Beyond that, she wanted to get past
this and see where things might go between her and
Russell. None of that would matter if the hit Simon
Griswold put out on her was allowed to succeed.

"Okay," she told the deputy marshal. "But I need
to tell Shailene I'm leaving. I owe her that much."

"All right." McDermott nodded. "Make it quick.
The longer this goes on in making yourself a target,
the more dangerous Nishimoto will be. For you, as
well as others."

Rosamund received the message, loud and clear.
She quickly tracked down her temporary boss, who
frowned at her, as though sensing something was up.

"What's going on?" Shailene asked.

"I have to leave," Rosamund responded straightforwardly. "I know the timing is terrible, but I'm in
trouble."

"What kind of trouble?" she pressed.

After a moment or two, Rosamund looked her in
the eye and said, thoughtful, "I'm a federal govern-
ment witness in a human trafficking case. I'll explain
more later. Right now, someone is trying to kill me."
She looked toward Patrick McDermott. "That's a deputy U.S. marshal, here to keep me safe—and every-

one in this restaurant. So, I need to go now, through the back door."

Shailene nodded understandingly. "Do what you need to do, Tisha." She paused, as if realizing that was not her real name. "Wouldn't want anything bad to happen to you. We'll hold the fort, somehow."

"Thanks, Shailene." Rosamund gave her a tiny, grateful smile and a quick hug, before hustling along with McDermott toward the back exit. In the process, she could only wonder if this was a move that Nishimoto had anticipated, possibly leaving them as lambs to be slaughtered by the hired killer.

Rosamund followed McDermott out the back door. He had removed from a shoulder holster his Glock 27 pistol. Following suit, in needing to feel useful in her own self-defense, she grabbed the Sig Sauer pistol from her ankle holster, while knowing that her cover life had been compromised. Staying low, while fearing she could be a sitting duck for Nishimoto, Rosamund peeled her eyes in every direction, wanting to at least give herself a fighting chance at surviving, should McDermott be taken out.

"No sign of him back here," the deputy marshal remarked.

"Not yet," she warned, realizing the merciless hitman could still have more than one trick up his sleeve.

"Stay down and close to the building," McDermott ordered. "I'm parked right around the corner and out of view of the apartment building."

"I hear you." Rosamund kept her voice to barely more than a whisper, for fear that Nishimoto may have planted listening devices in order to trap her. Or stay one step ahead of them.

Following closely behind McDermott, she made her way behind the back of the restaurant and other small businesses, before they came upon McDermott's Lincoln Corsair Reserve. "Get in," he said brusquely.

She quickly climbed into the passenger seat, after which McDermott closed the door, and raced to the driver's side, getting in and starting the car. "Let's get you out of here, before Nishimoto figures out that you're nowhere to be found at the restaurant and comes after you at Lynley's place."

"Okay." As they sped off on a side street, Rosamund felt relieved that she had stalled, at least temporarily, Griswold's hired assassin from carrying out the hit. But would that put Nishimoto off, angering him? Just as unsettling for her was the thought that he could accidentally or intentionally kill someone else in his quest and cold-heartedness. And where was Russell in all of this? Was he prepared to go toe to toe with a bona fide killer? Or would Russell allow those responsible for her safety to do the heavy lifting in going after Nishimoto?

All she could do was wait.

RUSSELL SPOTTED THE dark blue Mitsubishi Outlander Sport SE that Arnold Nishimoto was renting, using the alias Lyle Satoshige, parked on the street in front of the Liverwood Apartments. No one was inside. Russell only had to take one look to see that someone was on the roof of the apartment building across from Shailene's Grill. He saw just enough of the high-powered rifle to know that it was the hitman. Nishimoto's intention was to murder Rosamund through the window of the restaurant. No doubt the gunman had an escape route mapped out.

Sighing, Russell took solace in the knowledge that Rosamund had already vacated the restaurant under the protection of Deputy Marshal McDermott and been whisked off to the relatively safe location of Russell's own residence, awaiting word on how this went. Though he didn't believe that Nishimoto planned to kill patrons randomly, he didn't doubt that the hitman wouldn't hesitate to do so in going after Rosamund, viewing them as collateral damage.

Well, I won't let you harm a soul, least of all, Rosamund, Russell thought, while scaling the staircase to the roof of the apartment building. He knew that other law enforcement was en route and an effort was underway to quietly evacuate people from the area to be on the safe side. But he wasn't about to give Nishimoto an opportunity to escape the net and have Rosamund continuing to look over her shoulder, wondering when he would strike on behalf of his client.

Before opening the door that would take him to the rooftop, Russell removed his Glock 26 9-millimeter pistol from the belt holster, knowing it was loaded and ready to use. But he also knew he was dealing with a very dangerous man who had killed many people for hire, and quite possibly would prefer to go down swinging. If he went down at all.

I can't allow myself to worry about that, Russell told himself, willing to risk a gun battle that wouldn't necessarily go his way. This has to end now, if things between him and Rosamund were to have any real chance to prosper. He sucked in a deep breath and twisted the doorknob quietly. There was squeaking as the door opened and he stepped into the afternoon sunlight. To his left was an open and empty rifle case. To the right was the hired gun, dressed in black, down on one knee, and staring through the scope of a rifle that was perched on the ledge and aimed at Shailene's Grill below.

Russell took a few steps toward the perp, who surprisingly failed to hear him coming, so focused was he on nailing his prey. When close enough to serve his own purposes, Russell inhaled and stated in a deep voice, "Police! Arnold Nishimoto, drop the weapon. Now!"

Nishimoto, who was clearly startled, was defiant and wordless as he swung the rifle around to point it at Russell. But Russell never gave the hitman a chance to get off the first shot. He fired once, hitting Nishimoto squarely in the chin, and again, this one going into his left shoulder. Even as he went down like a sack of potatoes, the rifle flying from his outstretched hands, Nishimoto still appeared to reach for a handgun inside the waist of his pants. Russell recognized the weapon as a 38 S&W Special +P revolver. He kicked it away and placed the perp in handcuffs as Nishimoto fought to remain conscious.

When other law enforcement and paramedics arrived, Russell stepped aside and let them take over. Though he knew he would be put on administrative leave, pending a routine investigation into the shooting, Russell expected it to be fully justified in bringing down an armed and dangerous hired killer, while saving Rosamund's life as a result.

WHILE MCDERMOTT STOOD watch outside, Rosamund sat at the dining room table with her laptop and contacted Harold Paxton for a video chat. She needed to know what he thought about Simon Griswold's hitman, Arnold Nishimoto, having found her and what came next. When the special agent in charge's face appeared, he looked distressed, which wasn't surprising to Rosamund. "I suppose you've heard the latest news," she said.

"I know Nishimoto's been spotted in Weconta Falls," Paxton acknowledged grimly. "How the hell he managed to locate you is beyond me. The U.S. Marshals Service was supposed to be on top of providing you with a secure location till the trial."

Rosamund didn't disagree. "I'm sure they've done their best," she defended the USMS. "These things tend to happen sometimes."

"Shouldn't have happened this time, though," he barked.

"Maybe the mole within the organization is responsible for Nishimoto showing up," Rosamund suggested, knowing they had yet to identify the person and hold them accountable.

"That's highly unlikely," Paxton insisted. "Whoever has been leaking information would not have access to the USMS and WITSEC. If there is an inside job here, it would have to come from someone working within the U.S. Marshals Service. But that too is a stretch. My guess is that Arnold Nishimoto, an experienced hitman, likely used his skills to follow every lead and was somehow able to put two and two together in order to discover your whereabouts, in spite of the precautions taken to the contrary."

"So, what do we do about it?" Her tone was apprehensive. "How do we play this?"

"Right now, we do nothing to shake the apple cart, if you will," Paxton said with a direct look. "As I've been told, it appears that the locals have Nishimoto within their sights, with the feds closing in fast. My guess is that the threat he poses will soon be eradicated. If so, your status should remain the same and there will be no need to act."

Rosamund arched a brow. "And what if Nishimoto should remain on the loose and after me?" she asked, feeling ill at ease, knowing she couldn't remain there and feel comfortable about it.

"Then we'll reassess," the special agent in charge told her calmly. "Just know that your safety is our top priority within the DHS, Agent Santiago. We'll do whatever we need to do to stop Simon Griswold from silencing you before his trial begins. Let this play out and you'll get through it."

"All right." After they disconnected, in spite of his reassurances, Rosamund found herself still on pins and needles as she waited at Russell's house for word of what had happened after her pursuer attempted to kill her at Shailene's Grill. Had Arnold Nishimoto gotten away, prepared to wait for another day to track her down and complete his? Now that he had discovered her location and uncovered her identity, would she need to be renamed and moved to another safe space? If so, what would happen with her and Russell? She couldn't really expect him to follow her across the country, when he was content with his current life in Weconta Falls. Could she? Beyond that, if she was still to be a marked woman, would it be fair to him to be caught up in it? The one thing she would never want to see was Russell harmed and then have to live with it herself.

When he came through the door with Patrick Mc-Dermott, Russell looked exhausted, but otherwise unharmed. "Hey," he said to her, as she stood in the living room.

Rosamund responded in kind, "Hey." She tried to read his face but couldn't. "Tell me what happened with Nishimoto."

Russell ran a hand across his mouth, glanced at McDermott and then back to her, before announcing candidly, "The threat has been neutralized. Arnold Nishimoto is dead."

McDermott looked at Rosamund. "We were able to turn the tables on the hired killer," he said matter-of-factly.

"Yeah." Russell nodded. He faced Rosamund and said, "Nishimoto perched himself atop the apartment building across the street from Shailene's Grill. There, he intended to shoot you through the window when the opportunity presented itself. Which, of course, never materialized."

"Thank goodness, he didn't succeed," Rosamund stated deeply. She would never have forgiven herself had the hitman killed innocent people in the restaurant because of her.

Russell twisted his lips. "We believe that Nishimoto murdered Leah Redfield and tried to make it appear to be suicide."

Rosamund flinched at the thought, glancing at

McDermott and back. "All to get to me?" she asked
guiltily.

"None of this falls on you," Russell told her. "Like
all of us in law enforcement, Redfield assumed the
risks of being assigned as your handler. Undoubtedly, Nishimoto got the jump on her, but chances are
the DNA taken from Redfield's car will likely match
Nishimoto's DNA as circumstantial evidence, to go
with surveillance video, to link him to the crime."

"In the process, Leah didn't come away empty-
handed per se, in what I believe was her intention at
the end to somehow assist us in nailing her killer,"
McDermott said.

"Griswold's secret weapon in trying to squelch
your testimony against him has failed," Russell told
her. "You're safe now."

Rosamund fluttered her lashes, grateful to hear
this and happy that, even in the midst of a no-win
situation, Leah had managed to find a way through
getting the assassin to leave behind DNA evidence
to push back against Nishimoto's strategy. Still, Rosamund remained uneasy. Would Griswold simply
throw in the towel? Or try again to silence her? "Am
I really safe?" she had to ask.

Russell met her gaze. "Yes, if I have anything
to do with it," he assured her. "I won't let Griswold
get to you. If he gets another hired gun, we'll deal
with it and Griswold will fail again." He eyed Mc-
Dermott. "We're all on the same team here, with the

same objective—to keep you alive and well for your important role in taking down a human trafficking operation."

"Absolutely." The deputy marshal nodded in agreement. He grinned at her. "I'll leave you two alone and confer with my superiors on what the next move should be."

Rosamund smiled thinly. "Thanks for being there, Patrick," she said to him, as he had insisted that she refer to him by his first name.

"Just doing my job," he told her simply, and left.

Once they were alone, Russell held Rosamund's shoulders and reiterated, "It's going to be okay."

"I want to believe that," she uttered, looking into his eyes, while feeling his warmth.

"You should," he asserted and waited a beat. "Why don't I pour us some wine?"

"Okay." After they moved to the living room, Rosamund took a sip of wine and said, "Nishimoto must have been tipped off by someone on the inside about my whereabouts. Much like Simon Griswold knew about the undercover operation into his human trafficking organization, resulting in Johnnie's death. How else would Nishimoto have tracked me down?"

"You may be right," Russell agreed. "If so, between the DHS, HSI, and USMS, they'll have to figure it out, hopefully before Griswold goes to trial. But it's also possible that as a cutthroat and highly experienced assassin, Arnold Nishimoto was able to use all his skills and resources to discover your whereabouts all on his own. Either way, we stopped him from carrying out the hit."

"But will Griswold hire someone else to take Nishimoto's place?" She narrowed her eyes with speculation.

Russell came closer. "If so, we'll be ready to react to whatever comes our way," he said flatly.

"Oh, really?" Rosamund considered this. "You have your own life to live, Russell. Not to mention your duties with the Weconta Falls PD. I can't expect you to always be at my beck and call."

"Maybe I want to be," he countered boldly. "You mean enough to me to want to fight the good fight by your side. And as for my work as a police detective, I'm currently on administrative leave, pending the investigation into Nishimoto's death. While I'm confident of being cleared of any wrongdoing, it means I have some extra time on my hands to get to know the real you better, Rosamund Santiago. If that's all right with you?"

Rosamund could hardly say otherwise, wanting that as much as he did. "Yes, it's more than all right," she told him, forgetting about any hesitations on moving full steam ahead with their relationship. "I'd like that."

Russell smiled. "I was hoping you'd feel that way." He sealed the deal with a kiss that she happily joined in on.

Chapter Fourteen

"I think we both know this isn't where I belong," Russell told the police chief, as they sat in her office. It was exactly a month since the day he took out hired killer Arnold Nishimoto and two weeks since Russell was cleared of any wrongdoing. But it served as a wake-up call that his skills could be put to better use elsewhere. Not to mention, he needed to be closer to his long-distance girlfriend Rosamund Santiago, who was back in Dallas preparing for her testimony in the murder and human trafficking trial of Simon Griswold. Though she was supposed to be safeguarded by the DHS and HSI, Russell was still concerned that someone within those agencies may try to harm her. He believed the only way he would feel secure in her safety right now was if he was there by her side till this ordeal was over.

Diane O'Shea ran a hand through her hair. "I'd be lying if I said I expected you to stick around forever, Lynley," she admitted from the other side of her desk. "You obviously have too much going for you to want to remain a small-town detective, even at the senior level."

"Glad you understand." He had thought she might put up more of a fight to hang on to him. But it was better this way.

"I suppose you're headed back to the Bureau?"

"Probably." Though he hadn't made any definitive plans, it made the most sense to Russell. There still had to be an opening in the right place and, of course, a willingness on the part of the Bureau to take him back after his abrupt departure less than a year ago.

"Well, good luck to you," she voiced sincerely. "We'll miss you around here, but do what's best for you."

I intend to, Russell thought. "Thank you," he said. "I appreciate that you understand my situation."

Diane smiled. "But just so you know, if you ever get tired of big city crime and headaches, there will always be a place for you here."

He grinned. "I'll remember that."

Russell took a little time to say goodbye to his fellow detectives. "I'll miss you guys," he told Gloria and Ike, in particular, and meant it. They had become his family away from home.

"Yeah, right." Gloria rolled her eyes good-humoredly. "The moment you walk out that door, it'll be as though we never existed."

Ike was more envious when he said, "Maybe my time will come to pull up stakes and try something else."

"You never know," Russell told him. He smiled at Gloria. "I'll keep in touch, so I'll be sure to never forget you."

She smiled back. "Counting on that."

Once he was in his office, Russell packed his things and then opened his laptop for a video chat with Annette, the first of his siblings to hear the news of his official departure from the local PD.

Her eyes lit up. "You're just full of surprises," she teased him. "First your waitress girlfriend turns out to be a hotshot DHS special agent. Now you're looking for work again. What gives?"

He chuckled. "Well, what's life without a few twists and turns to keep things interesting?"

"Good point." She laughed. "So, when do I finally get to meet Rosamund face-to-face?"

Russell had already introduced her to all of his siblings and even a close cousin, Gavin Lynley, a special agent for the Mississippi Department of Corrections, Corrections Investigation Division, through a Zoom chat. In turn, he had gotten to meet by video Rosamund's parents, Julio and Theresa Santiago, and sister, Gabby. He looked forward to them all getting together in person one day. "Sometime after she testifies in the human trafficking case next week," he promised.

"Wonderful," Annette exclaimed. "Can't wait."

"Same here," he told her. After they disconnected, Russell checked in with Madison for a few minutes, got the scoop on her latest case and personal life; then called Scott, filling him in on the latest details of his life, before saying, "I think I want back in with the Bureau. Know anyone who can put in a good word or two for me?"

Scott laughed. "I think I may know someone who has a little pull in that regard."

"Good." Russell thought about syncing his work and private life with Rosamund, excited to be around her much more often.

"Welcome back to the Bureau," his brother voiced, perhaps prematurely. Russell liked hearing it all the same.

"I'll believe it when I see it," he half joked, fairly confident his former employer knew what he brought to the FBI's table. But for now, his only thought was to be in Dallas with Rosamund when she needed him most.

"You've got this, Rosamund," Special Agent Virginia Flannery, her new partner, said confidently.

"Oh, you think so, do you?" Rosamund said playfully. They were standing inside the Earle Cabell Federal Building on Commerce Street in Downtown Dallas, where she was to prep once more for the trial in a few days. With the threat to her safety diminished somewhat with the death of Arnold Nishimoto and Griswold's reach to access funds cut off, Rosamund had returned home, resuming her real identity.

Deputy U.S. Marshal Holly Kendall shadowed her every move. The thirty-eight-year-old African American single mother was tall and slender, with dark brown eyes and long hair in wavy brunette dreadlocks. Virginia was there to back up Holly, if need be.

Though Rosamund was happy to be back in her element as an HSI special agent, she missed not seeing Russell every day, in spite of their daily video chats when not with each other. They had agreed to try a long-distance romance, while striving to close the gap, one way or the other, in furthering their relationship. For her part, Rosamund remained open to being anywhere that could allow them to grow, while maintaining their careers. She knew that Russell's roots and siblings in law enforcement would keep him in the business, wherever his career took him; whereas her own dedication to stopping the scourge of human trafficking was important to her. Maybe she would be able to transfer to the Homeland Security Investigations San Francisco Field Office. Rosamund was determined to keep all options on the table, in the name of love and the chance at lasting happiness.

"I have confidence that you'll do just fine on the witness stand in nailing Simon Griswold," Virginia asserted. "Shouldn't take much to convince the assistant U.S. attorney for the Northern District of Texas, Laura Gibson-Norcross, of that."

"Hmm…" Rosamund smiled at her. "We shall see."

"I'll be out here when you're through," Holly said, after they had taken the elevator up to the third floor to the assistant U.S. attorney's office.

"Me too," Virginia added. "Unless I need to step away for a bit, with other duties still expected of me."

"Not a problem," Rosamund said, sure that Holly was more than up to the job, along with being able to defend herself, when push came to shove. Besides that, she knew Russell was flying in tomorrow, wanting to be there to offer his full support for the trial, and even serve as her bodyguard till then, if necessary.

When she stepped inside the office, Assistant U.S. Attorney Laura Gibson-Norcross greeted her, along with Harold Paxton. "Nice to see you again, Agent Santiago," she said with a pleasant smile, sticking out her hand.

"You too," Rosamund told her, smiling back as she took in the attractive fortysomething attorney, with short, fine blond hair in a piecey style and close-set green eyes. She was wearing a tailored periwinkle skirt suit and black pumps. Rosamund shook her hand.

"Special Agent Santiago," Paxton said, and put forth a large hand, which she shook too.

"Agent Paxton," she said, never feeling comfortable calling him Harold, as he had given her permission to do.

"Why don't we all have a seat," Laura said, extending her thin arm toward a set of upholstered task chairs around a cherry conference table near a wall with windows. Once they were seated, she clasped her hands and spoke candidly, "I think we can all agree that human trafficking and its components, human smuggling, sexual exploitation, and slavery, have no place in our state. It's imperative that we use everything at our disposal to stop this from happening." She eyed Rosamund. "Your testimony against Simon Griswold is key to putting a serious dent in this criminality in and around Dallas, while sending a clear message to other human traffickers that this won't be tolerated here and offenders will be prosecuted to the fullest extent of the law."

Rosamund nodded solemnly. "I'm happy to do my part in the fight against human trafficking in Texas," she stressed.

"You've gone well beyond the call of duty, Agent Santiago," Paxton told her. "After the ordeal you've been put through, including the tragic death of our fallen agent Johnnie Langford, and surviving not one, but two assassination attempts, I'd say you've earned your stripes within Homeland Security Investigations, and then some."

"Thank you, Sir," Rosamund said. She quickly got over the praise, though, knowing that any HSI or DHS special agents would do the same thing while performing their duties, and told the special agent in charge as much. She added humbly, "The important thing, as Assistant U.S. Attorney Gibson-Norcross indicated, is that we have to go after the human traffickers with everything we've got, so women, children, and even men can stop being illegally brought across the border or coerced into forced labor, commercial sexual exploitation, and other forms of involuntary actions."

Laura nodded appreciatively. "Well said, Agent Santiago. You're definitely a real asset to DHS and its Center for Countering Human Trafficking." She smiled, glancing briefly at Paxton, before saying, "Now, let's go over your testimony in the trial of Simon Griswold."

Rosamund didn't hold back in responding in detail to everything she knew about Griswold's human trafficking organization, including recruitment methods, pressure tactics, relocating, drugging, and sexually exploiting those impacted, and even committing murder as part of keeping members and trafficking victims in line. When it was over, both Laura and Paxton agreed that she was ready to testify against Griswold and that testimony, combined with hard evidence against the trafficker, would all but certainly lead to a conviction and the dismantling of his network.

On the way back to Rosamund's house, Holly Kendall asked her, "So, how did it go in there?"

"As well as could be expected," she responded, looking at the deputy marshal, who was behind the wheel of a blue Subaru Outback Wilderness. Driving behind them was Virginia in her white Ford Escape Hybrid. "I'm all set for the trial," Rosamund declared.

Holly grinned. "Well, good for you."

"Once this is over, I hope we can still hang out together sometime." Like Leah Redfield and Patrick McDermott before her, Rosamund liked having Holly around.

"Of course," Holly responded enthusiastically. "I'd like that too."

"Cool." Rosamund smiled, and imagined that, along with Virginia, the three could have some girls' nights out. Of course, she was more interested in spending as much time with Russell as their schedules allowed. Neither of them had spoken about tying the knot. For her part, Rosamund knew she loved him and wanted that. She suspected Russell felt the same, but both wanted to wait till after the trial to decide where they wanted to live before making any other plans.

They arrived at Rosamund's two-bedroom, split-level loft condominium on Mockingbird Lane, where Rosamund had lived for more than a year before the relocation to witness protection. It was in a recently renovated warehouse and had a fitness center and twenty-four-hour security patrol. The loft had vaulted ceilings, vinyl plank flooring, a gourmet kitchen with an open concept, and floor-to-ceiling fiberglass windows that offered amazing views of the city, with the loft's proximity to Uptown Dallas. She had filled it with bamboo furnishings and felt the loft was a good fit for a single woman. But with Russell now in her life, Rosamund wondered if it would suffice for them as a couple, should they decide to live together in the city.

That thought was put on hold as she enjoyed a glass of white wine with Holly and Virginia, while standing around the quartz countertop island in the kitchen. They talked about their lives, ups and downs, and future prospects. When Virginia's cell phone rang, she answered, listened, and then said grimly, "I'm on my way."

"What is it?" Rosamund asked uneasily.

"A search warrant has been issued for the home of a person suspected of possessing child pornography." Virginia furrowed her brow. "They want me in on it, so I have to go." She paused. "Hate to leave you high and dry, Rosamund."

"I'll be fine," she responded. "Holly is still here, and I wouldn't be surprised if more marshals showed up between now and the trial date. So go."

Holly eyed Virginia and echoed the sentiments. "I have a job to do and won't let anything happen to Rosamund to prevent her from testifying."

"I get it." Virginia made a face. "It's just like you two to gang up on me."

Rosamund chuckled. "I'll see you when I see you," she said, as she ushered her to the door.

No sooner had she settled down on the bamboo sectional with Holly, when the doorbell rang. Rosamund wondered if it was Russell, who wasn't supposed to arrive till the next day. She'd also given him a key. Maybe Virginia was back already, no longer needed for the mission.

"I'll go check it out," Holly said guardedly. "Stay here."

Rosamund remained seated and watched as the deputy marshal looked through the peephole before recognizing the visitor. "It's your boss," she said, and opened the door.

Harold Paxton came inside, looking flustered. "There's been a breach in security," he told them, and gazed at Rosamund. "We need to get you to a safe house till we can make sure this has been resolved satisfactorily."

"Okay." Rosamund stood up, feeling this must be serious, as it was the first time she had been visited in person by the special agent in charge of the HSI Dallas Field Office.

"I'll call it in," Holly said.

"No time for that," he insisted. "We need to go. Now! We'll take my car, as Simon Griswold's operatives will be looking for your official vehicle, Deputy Marshal Kendall."

Rosamund barely had time to grab her cell phone before leaving with Paxton and Holly. Inadvertently left behind was Rosamund's Sig Sauer striker-fired pistol.

Chapter Fifteen

After arriving at the Dallas Fort Worth International Airport, Russell grabbed his charcoal carry-on spinner luggage from the overhead compartment in first class and went to the rental car office to rent a Nissan Rogue. He called Rosamund to surprise her that he decided to come in a day early and should be at her place shortly. Moreover, he wanted to remind her that once he put his house up for sale shortly, they would never need to be apart again if he had anything to do with it. When she didn't pick up, he left her a text message to that effect. Though he had no reason in particular to believe there was anything to be concerned about, warning bells went off in Russell's head. Something wasn't right. Call it a gut feeling or a greater sense of dread that everything seemed to be going almost too well since Rosamund returned to Dallas. Not that he wasn't happy this was the case. But what if it was a false read, meant for people like him to let down their guard, so Rosamund could be prevented from testifying against Simon Griswold with little to no resistance? Just because Arnold Nishimoto was no longer in the picture didn't make Griswold any less dangerous in his desperation to keep from spending the rest of his life in prison.

Am I overreacting? Russell had to ask himself as he got on the road. Maybe his deep love for Rosamund and strong desire to give her the type of great life she deserved as his wife and mother of their future children was clouding his judgment. Or maybe his instincts were spot on. Wasn't there still an unnamed mole at the DHS or HSI? What if this person was gunning for Rosamund and found a way to get to her on behalf of Griswold or in conjunction with him?

When he got to her loft, Russell let himself in, hoping to find Rosamund there with the armed deputy marshal to protect her. And maybe Rosamund's partner, Virginia Flannery. Instead, the place was empty. He noted empty wineglasses in the kitchen. But nothing seemed out of order. Where was she?

Russell texted her again with no response. This left him even more alarmed. He tried calling Virginia, who answered right away. "Hi," she said spiritedly.

"I'm here at Rosamund's loft and she's nowhere to be found," he stated. "Not picking up when I call her or responding to texts. Do you know where she is?"

"Hmm…" Virginia sounded baffled. "When I left a little while ago, she and Holly, the deputy marshal, were still there."

"Did Rosamund mention anywhere that she planned to go?"

"Not that I can recall. I just assumed she was going to stay there for the evening." She paused. "You think something may have happened to her?"

Russell stiffened. "You tell me."

"Why don't I call Holly and see what she has to say," Virginia suggested.

"Please do," he urged her. "And send me Holly's cell phone number while you're at it."

After texting him the number and putting him on hold for a moment, Virginia came back on and said, "She's not picking up either."

Trying to remain calm, Russell asked her suspiciously, "So, why aren't you with them?"

"I was sent on another assignment," she explained.

"By whom?"

"Harold Paxton, the special agent in charge of the Dallas Field Office."

Russell mused about that. Why would Paxton want to take Rosamund's partner off helping to safeguard her this close to the trial of Simon Griswold? What was up with that? Was it a deliberate plan on his part to reduce the number of people present at the loft to Rosamund and Holly, thereby leaving Rosamund more vulnerable? "Did Paxton offer to add more agents or marshals to Rosamund's security detail?"

"No," she admitted. "I think he thought Holly would be enough security for now—at least till the day of the trial." Virginia took a breath. "What are you thinking?"

"That Rosamund may be in trouble and, if so, Paxton's involved," Russell said, making his feelings clear.

"He wouldn't hurt her," she insisted. "Harold's the special agent in charge, for crying out loud. Why would he want to stop Rosamund from testifying?"

"That's a good question." Russell jutted his chin pensively. "When I have an answer, I'll let you know. Meanwhile, I'd appreciate it if this conversation stays between us for the time being." He sensed that she could be trusted, even if placing Paxton on a proverbial pedestal.

"Of course," Virginia agreed, and added, "I'm coming over there."

"Good," he said. "If Rosamund shows up, let me know."

"Where are you going?"

"To have a look around." Russell disconnected. He left the condo and headed down to a lobby area, where he noted the security cameras. He needed to see under what circumstances Rosamund had left and if it was of her own accord. Making his way to a small office on the property, Russell acted with authority, despite currently being between jobs, when he requested to the twentysomething woman on duty that he take a look at the surveillance footage.

Batting brown eyes, Mary Heard flipped back her long and layered ginger-colored hair before playing the video. When she came to the part where Rosamund showed up, Russell asked Mary to stop. He noted that Rosamund was next to Holly. A man was behind them, but clearly with them.

"Let's zoom in on the man there," Russell directed.

"Okay."

He recognized him as Harold Paxton, Rosamund's boss and the special agent in charge, as Russell had made a point of familiarizing himself somewhat with those in her inner circle with the HSI. Where was Paxton taking Rosamund and why? Was there a threat to her safety that he hadn't bothered to inform Virginia of? Or did he have something more ominous in mind in sending Rosamund's partner off to another assignment?

Russell left the office and got on the phone with his brother, Scott. "Rosamund's missing," he told him, recognizing that his suspicions were unsubstantiated at this point.

"Missing?" Scott repeated. "Explain?"

Russell filled him in, coming back to Harold Paxton. "I need you to see if there have been any red flags there, be it professionally or personally."

"I'll check him out," Scott promised. "But there could be a perfectly reasonable explanation as to why Rosamund's not responding to your calls or texts," he cautioned.

"I know," Russell allowed. "But my instincts are telling me otherwise." And in this case, that was something he couldn't afford to ignore. Not when Rosamund's very survival could well be on the line.

ROSAMUND WAS IN the front passenger seat as Paxton drove his maroon Chrysler Pacifica Pinnacle to a single-story farmhouse on Jamaica Street in the Southeast Dallas section of the city. It was at the end of a street lined with dogwood trees. She felt a bit uneasy about the situation and naked without her duty weapon, but counted on the special agent in charge and Holly, who was in the back seat, to keep her safe till more help arrived.

They exited the vehicle, with Paxton leading the way. While approaching the house, he said in a calm voice, "Nothing will happen to you here."

While she wanted to believe that, there was a coldness in his green eyes that made Rosamund wonder if there was something he was keeping from them. She glanced at Holly, who also seemed to have reservations. The moment they stepped inside the living room and onto the red oak hardwood flooring, Rosamund noted the space was sparsely furnished. The room was somewhat dark and the teal curtains were drawn on all the windows.

It was only when she looked into a corner did Rosamund notice what appeared to be a body lying on the floor. In a matter of seconds, she was able to assess that it was a slender adult male of short stature with dark hair in a mohawk fade style and a short,

boxed beard. He was wearing faded jeans, a jersey
T-shirt, and dark sneakers. Gasping, she turned on
Paxton, just as Holly was saying with an edge to her
voice, "What happened to him?"

Paxton was now holding in a gloved hand a gun—in
what looked to Rosamund to be a compact 9-millimeter
piece—and aimed it at them. "He's dead," the special
agent in charge replied brusquely. "He is—or was—
my informant, Leo Neuman. I killed him. Right after
he killed you, Deputy Marshal." Before Holly could
remove her firearm from the belly band holster inside
her flare-leg pants, Paxton shot her in the chest. Instinctively, she put a hand to the spot where the bullet
entered, before losing consciousness and falling onto
her back. With lightning speed, he raced over to her
and grabbed her Glock 27 pistol and faced Rosamund,
before she could make a move. "Don't even think about
it," he warned her, pointing his gun at her. "Not unless
you're ready to die too…"

Rosamund weighed her options, which were little
to none, without having her own firearm. She wanted
to go to Holly's aide, hoping she could somehow hold
on. But Paxton was clearly not interested in helping
someone he had just shot in cold blood.

"Actually," Paxton said with a wry chuckle, "you
should already be dead, Agent Santiago. Right alongside your late partner, Langford."

Rosamund's eyes widened. "What?"

"That's right, you should also be dead and buried, had Simon Griswold been more competent in his ability to shoot you when he had the chance. But his gun had to lock at the worst possible time for him." Paxton grimaced. "Griswold certainly can't blame me for his current predicament. I handed you and Langford to him on a silver platter. It was up to Griswold to finish you both off."

"You're the mole?" Rosamund's voice cracked. How could this be?

"You got me," Paxton confessed brashly.

She glared at him. "Why?" she asked pointedly, while trying to wrap her mind around the notion that her boss could be a crook and killer, all wrapped in one.

"Griswold paid me handsomely to look the other way," he contended. "I needed the money for various reasons. But I also needed to make the efforts to go after Griswold and his human trafficking organization seem believable. So, I sent you and Langford in undercover, hoping you would do little more than scratch the surface to go after a few underlings. But you got too close and Griswold needed to know about it. Or it would ruin the good thing we had going between us."

"Does that mean it was you who also exposed me to Griswold's hitman, Arnold Nishimoto?" she asked, still in shock.

"Right again." Paxton laughed, while still aiming the gun at her, his hand steady. "It was Griswold's idea to put a hit out on you. I went along with it because I didn't want your testimony to blow back on me and my career with the DHS. Though the U.S. Marshals Service was a tough nut to crack in giving you a new identity and place to live that was not directly accessible to me apart from phone communication, I was finally able to pin it down and give Nishimoto everything he needed to finish you off once and for all. But, like Griswold, he failed, leaving me to clean up his mess before this goes to trial and the assistant U.S. attorney puts you on the stand to tell everything you know about Simon Griswold. After that, it wouldn't take long before Laura figured out my role and came after me. I can't allow that."

Rosamund was almost speechless. He had betrayed his office in the HSI and his integrity as a human being. And for what? Profit and greed. Now he had blood on his hands and Paxton fully intended to get them bloodier by killing her. And he was in a good enough position that he just might be able to pull it off, Rosamund feared.

"Your phone?" Paxton demanded, holding out one hand, while keeping the gun on her with the other. "Toss it over. And don't try anything funny, Agent Santiago. Or I'll kill you on the spot!"

Though it pained Rosamund to obey his command by giving up her one lifeline, with Paxton having her at a serious disadvantage, she had no choice but to comply. She could only hope that by keeping it turned on throughout this ordeal, there was still time for her location to be tracked. She slid the phone from the back pocket of her pants, then tossed it on the floor near him.

Paxton then stomped on the phone till it broke. He chuckled wickedly. "Afraid no one can come to your rescue now."

Rosamund was of the same mind, but refused to give in to what seemed like an inevitable fate.

"THERE ARE NO red flags, per se," Scott told him, as Russell listened to him over the speakerphone, while driving around the city.

"Tell me more about the per se," he said intently.

"Well, there were rumors when Paxton was the deputy special agent in charge of the field office in Albuquerque that he had a problem with gambling and had accrued debts in relation to that. But this was never proven, so he kept his career going."

"If he was a gambling addict and maybe still is, that would open the door to Paxton seeking out ways to fund his habit," Russell put forth. "Including aligning himself with the likes of Simon Griswold."

"Certainly can't rule it out," Scott said, "even if that would be taking things to the extreme, if Paxton were to risk everything for essentially nothing."

"Isn't that always the case for desperate people?" Russell pursed his lips. "Paxton was clearly in a position to finger Rosamund and Langford in a deal with the devil. When it only resulted in eliminating half the problem, Paxton could also have ratted out Rosamund to Nishimoto to keep Rosamund from breaking up the profitable party. I'm just saying." He could barely believe this was possible himself. But it made sense on another level. And Russell knew that bad people came from all walks of life. Including possibly within the ranks of the U.S. Department of Homeland Security.

"You'll find her," his brother said quietly.

"Yeah." Russell wanted to believe that with all his heart. Anything less would be unthinkable. He saw that his cell phone was buzzing, and that it was Virginia. "I have another call I need to take," he told Scott.

"Okay." He waited a beat. "Keep me posted."

"I will." Russell disconnected and put Virginia on the line. "Is Rosamund there?" He hoped that all his worry and condemning Harold Paxton was much ado about nothing.

"Afraid not," Virginia replied soberly. "But I think I know where she is."

"Where?" He crossed over an intersection.

"A safe house we use sometimes when working with informants," she said. "I'd almost forgotten that I installed a GPS tracker on Rosamund's cell phone at her request. I checked and it shows her phone was at that address. Till it went dead."

Russell tensed in considering that last part. Why

would her phone go dead? Was it off? Or disabled by someone who wanted to make it unusable? He told her that Rosamund and Holly left the loft with Paxton and asked what he already knew the answer to, "Does he regularly deal with witnesses directly in this way?"

"Not that I've seen," Virginia admitted.

"Didn't think so. I think he targeted Rosamund and sent you in another direction to buy himself some time."

"Maybe Harold saw a security threat and acted upon it, knowing how vital a witness Rosamund is?" she suggested.

"Maybe, but my gut is telling me otherwise." Russell sucked in a deep breath. "What's the address to the safe house?"

She gave it and said, "I'm heading over there too."

"Whatever you do, don't let Paxton know we're coming," Russell stressed. "If he gets wind of it, there's no telling what he might do if desperate enough."

"Got it."

"You might want to call for backup and an ambulance, in case someone's hurt," he told her, fearful that Paxton might already have harmed Rosamund or Holly.

"Will do," Virginia said.

He disconnected and used the car's navigation system to guide him to the safe house. He put on the speed, knowing that every second counted, if he were to get there in time to save the woman he loved.

"So, what, you plan to shoot me and try to pin it on the person over there?" Rosamund glanced at the dead man in the corner.

Paxton grinned as he kept the gun on her. "Actually, the way this is going to work, Agent Santiago, is that my dead informant shot you and Deputy Marshal Kendall with this gun, having done so in betraying me in some misguided attempt to help out an innocent Simon Griswold. I then had no choice but to shoot the informant, Leo Neuman, with my official firearm in my own self-defense." He laughed at the absurdity of it all.

"You're not going to be able to get away with this," Rosamund told him, if only to buy some extra time, knowing it was running out fast.

"I already have," Paxton bragged. "You see, once this is over, I'll be able to sell the DHS and the assistant U.S. attorney on what went down, much to their chagrin, but believable nonetheless. With you dead, the case against Griswold falls apart and we get to go back to a mutually profitable arrangement." He chortled. "Nice working with you, Agent Santiago, but all good things must come to an end. At least for you. No lucky gun jamming this time around to save you, I'm afraid."

With nowhere left to turn and nothing to lose at this point, Rosamund lunged at Paxton, catching him off guard just long enough to grab his wrist and twist it violently, before he could shoot her. The gun flew out of his hand. As he howled like a wounded animal, Paxton was able to recover enough to use his other fist to slam it hard into her cheek, causing Rosamund to see stars.

"You've got guts, Agent Santiago, I'll give you that," Paxton voiced, ignoring his own pain. "But this is still only going to end one way."

"Maybe not the way you think," Rosamund retorted, as he swung another fist at her face, which she dodged and then went to some Thai boxing moves. She hit his face squarely between the eyes, grabbed his waist and rammed a knee solidly into his groin, then smashed a fist into his thick neck. Though he groaned with discomfort, Paxton used his greater size and strength to lift her off the floor and throw her against the wall. Rosamund grimaced from the pain and tried to clear her head, as she sensed that he was ready to move in for the kill. Was she still up for a fight for survival? Or had he already won the battle?

Chapter Sixteen

When he entered the house, Russell wasn't sure what to expect. All he knew was that if Rosamund was still alive, he would make sure she stayed that way. He noted right away an unidentified male and the deputy marshal Holly Kendall on the floor. Neither were moving and both appeared to have been shot.

Russell turned to his left and saw Rosamund against a wall and Harold Paxton ready to charge at her like a raging bull. By the looks of him, he had taken some punishment. But not enough to bring him to his knees. Russell was not about to let him hurt her any more than he may already have. Before Paxton could reach Rosamund, Russell caught up to him and grabbed his arm, swinging him around to face him. "I'd like to get in on the action, Paxton," Russell told him.

Paxton yelled an expletive and went into fight mode. Russell was more than happy to mix it up, as he went to town on the special agent in charge. Heavy blows to both cheeks and chin were thrown by

Russell as Paxton flailed away, mostly at air, before he went down in a heap, passing out cold.

After putting handcuffs on Paxton, Russell went over to Rosamund and held her shoulders. "Are you okay?" he asked gingerly.

"I'll live," she told him honestly, but winced to let him know she was experiencing some aches and pains.

He nodded. "Glad to hear that."

"Holly…" Rosamund's voice cracked as she raced over to the deputy marshal. She was still unconscious and bleeding from the gunshot wound. Rosamund put a hand to her neck and detected a faint pulse. "She's alive!"

"Help is on the way," Russell told her, lifting Rosamund up.

She met his eyes. "I was afraid I'd never see you again."

"That was never going to happen," he insisted in a soothing tone. He hid his own fear that he might have lost her.

"How did you find me?" she asked curiously. "Especially since you weren't even supposed to arrive in Dallas till tomorrow."

"Virginia was able to track your location through the GPS tracker on your phone," Russell explained, "giving me something to work with." He added, "As for being in town, I decided to come a day sooner." He'd tell her about his employment status later.

Rosamund smiled gratefully. "Good thing."

"So, what happened here with Paxton?" Russell asked anxiously.

She drew a breath, glancing at the knocked-out special agent in charge. "He was in cahoots with Simon Griswold," she explained. "Paxton was the mole in the DHS by way of the HSI. He wanted both me and Johnnie dead so we wouldn't spoil the arrangement Paxton had with Griswold, who paid him blood money to bypass any serious investigation into Griswold's human trafficking enterprise. When I survived, Paxton worked with Griswold to take the hit out on me. Paxton fed Arnold Nishimoto the information on my whereabouts to finish the job and prevent me from testifying."

"And when that failed, Paxton went after you himself," Russell muttered, his brow creased with anger.

"Yes," Rosamund said with dismay. "He killed his informant and shot Holly, intending to set up the informant for our deaths, so Paxton could get Griswold off the hook."

"But it blew up in his face," Russell said.

"Looks that way."

As they mulled that over, Virginia showed up and embraced Rosamund. "You're alive!" she uttered happily.

"No thanks to him." Rosamund eyed their boss, who was still unconscious. "He tried to kill me… and Holly…"

Virginia frowned sullenly, glancing at the gravely

injured deputy marshal. "The ambulance should be here any minute now."

"Good," Rosamund said, "I can only hope that Holly will pull through."

Paramedics arrived and Holly was stabilized, before being taken to the hospital, still alive. Soon the safe house was crawling with law enforcement and crime scene investigators, while Harold Paxton, battered and bruised, was placed under arrest on a slew of charges.

"It's over now," Russell said comfortingly, wrapping Rosamund in his arms as they stood outside.

"Not quite," she reminded him. "There's still my testimony that's needed to put Simon Griswold away for life."

"True." Russell took a breath. "And Harold Paxton will be joining him behind bars for a very long time," he stated confidently. "It's been rumored that Paxton had a gambling problem over the years that may have caused him to cross the line."

"Excuses, excuses." Rosamund wrinkled her nose unsympathetically toward her former boss. "For Johnnie, Leah, and Holly, I hope he rots in jail."

"He will," Russell asserted, knowing there was no way out of this for Paxton. He realized that, for Rosamund, seeing the man she once looked up to pay the price for his criminality would be one big source of satisfaction. With another being the dismantling of Simon Griswold's human trafficking business and with that, less victimization of innocent children, women, and men as a result. "Let's go home," Russell told her, feeling that this really would be home for him, or wherever Rosamund wanted to be, now that his time in Weconta Falls had come to an end.

"So, I QUIT my job," Russell said to Rosamund that evening, as if it was a routine thing, as he sat beside her on the sectional in her loft, a bottle of beer in hand. She had been debriefed by the various powers that be as was standard procedure in a federal investigation of this magnitude. The replacement deputy U.S. marshal Joel Elizondo, a tall and thick-set forty-year-old with walnut-colored eyes and dark hair in a Caesar cut, stood guard outside the door, just in case there was more trouble. Holly Kendall had gone into surgery immediately and everything had gone well according to doctors, with the belief among them that Holly would miraculously make a full recovery. Virginia was home, but just a phone call away, if needed.

"Seriously?" Rosamund's eyes widened with surprise. They had talked about one or the other shifting careers to be together, but nothing definitive.

"Yeah, I'm officially no longer Detective Lynley, Weconta Falls Police Department." He grinned and sipped the beer. "Getting out of Dodge," he joked. "Put the house on the market and, hopefully, it will sell soon."

"Are you sure about this?" she had to ask, knowing it was probably too late to have a redo. She sipped her own beer.

"How can I not be?" he responded coolly. "It wouldn't have been fair to ask you to give up what you do, given your dedication to the job. In fact, once the trial is over, I wouldn't be surprised if you got a promotion to move up the ladder with the DHS or Homeland Security Investigations."

"I wish." Rosamund tsked, not wanting to get ahead of herself in merely doing her duties, hazardous and all. "But anyway, this is about you," she told him, feeling a little guilty that he was suddenly unemployed. "What will you do now?" With his law enforcement résumé, she was sure he would find gainful employment soon.

"Actually, I'm about to rejoin the Bureau," Russell uttered proudly.

"Really?" She gazed at him with excitement. "That was quick."

"I've been thinking about it for a while," he admitted. "Even before you came into my life, truthfully, I was starting to feel a little restless, wondering if I could ever settle for small-town detective work when there were so many interesting assignments potentially awaiting me with the FBI. I'm ready to get back in the saddle, if you will. Scott seems to think that it's more or less a done deal. I'll take him at his word for that. Unless I find out otherwise, I should be reemployed with the Bureau in no time flat. In the meantime, I'm here to support you every step of the way as you put the screws to Simon Griswold and his new jail pal, Harold Paxton."

"Thank you," Rosamund gushed, eager to put this case and those bad actors in the rearview mirror, so her focus could instead be more on the evolving relationship between her and Russell. "Just know that the support works both ways," she stressed.

"I do know that." He grinned and kissed her. "I also know that I love doing that."

She blushed, touching her tingling mouth. "And I love you doing it," she said. "Along with kissing you back."

"Anytime you like," he challenged her.

Rosamund didn't disappoint. "How about now and forever," she teased him.

He grinned. "Works for me."

As it did for her. She kissed him and let it linger for a while, welcoming the respite from escaping death more than once and readying herself for the big day in court.

ON THE FIRST day of the trial, Rosamund entered the Earle Cabell Federal Building, accompanied by Russell, Virginia, Deputy U.S. Marshal Joel Elizondo, and Rosamund's sister, Gabby Ulrich, who flew in the night before to show her support. Gabby was basically a slightly younger version of herself, Rosamund felt, only an inch shorter with long, straight dark hair with cappuccino highlights.

"I know you'll do great," Gabby encouraged her, after they were brought to a waiting room till it was time for Rosamund to testify.

"Absolutely," Russell agreed. "You're well prepared to take whatever Griswold's attorney throws at you."

"Thanks." Rosamund welcomed the confidence they showed in her and was happy to see that two of the most important people in her life seemed to have hit it off. She looked forward to meeting Russell's siblings in person. "I'll do my best," she promised, knowing her testimony could make or break the federal case against Simon Griswold. She fully expected that she would also be called upon to testify against Harold Paxton, once he went to trial for murder, attempted murder, money laundering, and other serious charges.

"And I'll be there with you every step of the way," Virginia pitched in, as someone also slated to testify later regarding her investigation into Griswold's human trafficking operation while Rosamund was under the federal program.

"I know," she said, smiling at her partner. Before she could contemplate further, Rosamund received word that it was time, as she was being called as the first witness.

She received a warm hug from Russell, who whispered in her ear, "Good luck."

Her eyes crinkled as she whispered back, "That's already come in meeting you."

"I feel the same," he promised with a grin, while looking dapper in a gray suit and black loafers.

She took that to heart and left the room, where Rosamund was led to the courtroom by Deputy Marshal Joel Elizondo. He'd been shaken up by the near-death experience of his colleague Holly Kendall, and was determined to do his part to look after Holly's two children till she recovered.

Rosamund wore a navy blue houndstooth-print skirt suit and black pumps as she made her way toward the witness box. Her hair, which had started to grow out, was in a twisted updo. She looked at Laura Gibson-Norcross, who would be questioning her. Laura flashed her a soft smile. Next to Laura at the prosecutors table was fellow assistant U.S. Attorney Neil Rivera, who was thirtysomething, very tall, lean, and bald-headed. He also acknowledged Rosamund.

She turned to the defendant, Simon Griswold. He wore a charcoal gray suit, and she noted his pompadour fade hairstyle was now grayer. Next to him was his attractive attorney, Alicia Aotaki, whose long brunette hair was in a bubble ponytail. Griswold favored Rosamund with a menacing stare before she looked away, determined not to let him get to her. On the contrary, she was more than ready to do her part to put Griswold away for life, in memory of her late partner, Johnnie Langford, and for the many victims of Griswold's human trafficking.

Rosamund took the stand, steeling herself for what was to come. Laura Gibson-Norcross left her table and approached confidently, as she offered Rosamund another supportive smile, then said respectfully, "Agent Santiago, why don't we start with you telling us who you work for?"

"I work for the United States Department of Homeland Security," Rosamund told her.

"And what is it that you do for the DHS?" she asked.

"I'm a Homeland Security Investigations special agent in its Center for Countering Human Trafficking."

Laura waited a beat and continued, "Tell us a bit about what your duties entail?"

Rosamund adjusted in the seat and went through the CCHT's mission of countering the crimes involving human trafficking, protecting and rescuing victims, and increasing deterrence efforts, using the DHS's strengths and resources, often in cooperation with its partners in law enforcement across the country. "Our entire goal is to stop the trafficking of humans through all the legal means at our disposal, saving lives in the process," she concluded.

Again, the assistant U.S. attorney allowed that to sink in before saying evenly, "Let's turn to your purpose for being a witness for the prosecution today, Agent Santiago." Laura glared at the defendant and turned back to Rosamund. "Why don't you tell us about your mission as an undercover agent that led to this very moment in time."

Rosamund sucked in a deep breath and met the cold stare of Simon Griswold, who had tried to kill her twice, one of which was by his own hand. She had cheated death both times and now had the opportunity for justice to be served. She was more than up to the task. She was determined to make sure he paid for his terrible crimes and for snubbing his nose at the laws of the country he lived in for profit and total disregard for anyone but himself. Similar to his partner in crime, Harold Paxton.

RUSSELL QUIETLY SLIPPED into a seat in the spectator section and listened in as Rosamund took it to Simon Griswold, detailing his sordid human trafficking operation and various means of coercing, recruiting, capturing, and separating victims for forced labor, sexual exploitation, and sex slavery. She withstood a withering cross-examination by the defense lawyer, as Rosamund more than held her ground in making the case against Griswold.

During the afternoon session, it was much of the same as Rosamund testified with grit and determination. When it was time to point the finger at Griswold for the murder of Johnnie Langford, she didn't hold back.

"The defendant, Simon Griswold, showed no hesitation or mercy when he pulled the trigger of his gun and shot to death my partner, Homeland Security Investigations Special Agent Johnnie Langford, at point-blank range," Rosamund recounted, grimacing at the painful memory. "Were it not for the defendant's firearm jamming, I wouldn't be here in this courtroom today." She sighed. "But I am here and doing the right thing by exposing the defendant for the monster he truly is."

Russell could see that the jury was moved by her testimony, which was met with approval by the prosecutors. It made him love Rosamund all the more, knowing what kind of a woman he was getting as a romantic partner and, hopefully, future wife and mother of his children. When her testimony was finished, Rosamund left the witness stand with her head held high, after giving everything she had toward securing a conviction for Griswold. Russell was proud of her and more than ready to begin the next chapter of their lives together.

Two WEEKS LATER, the jury returned a guilty verdict against Simon Griswold, who would be spending the rest of his life behind bars. And with this, her round-the-clock security was no longer needed. Rosamund celebrated the verdict with Russell over dinner at one of her favorite restaurants, Eve's Steak Castle, on Main Street in Downtown Dallas.

"We did it!" she declared, raising her goblet of red wine triumphantly, while feeling good knowing that

Griswold would never again be able to practice the trading of humans for commercial sexual exploitation, forced labor, and other illicit purposes.

"Never doubted you would," Russell said coolly, cutting into his filet mignon. "Between your testimony and the strong evidence the feds had going for them, it was evident that Griswold was going down. It was just a matter of time, which for him has now run out."

Rosamund smiled. "Thank goodness for that." She forked a slice of her Wagyu strip steak. "Next up is Harold Paxton," she stated. "I hear they're throwing the book at him, and deservedly so."

"I'll say." Russell took a sip of his wine. "He's the worst of the worst in using his position of authority to profit off victims of trafficking, even to the point of being willing to kill to continue lining his pockets."

She twisted her lips at the thought of the former special agent in charge attempting to murder her, and very nearly succeeding. But she wasn't about to let that spoil the evening and spending quality time with the man she loved. When Rosamund looked at him, she realized that Russell was staring at her across the booth. "What?" she asked, wondering if she had stained her floral appliqué midi dress with food or something.

"Well, I have news," he began mysteriously.

She eyed him musingly. "What news might that be?"

Russell sat back. "Thought you might like to know

that I'm officially back with the Bureau," he said. "We still need to iron out a few minor details but, as of now, I'm a full-fledged FBI special agent again."

Rosamund smiled. "That's terrific!" She knew he had been working toward this and even considered other options, had it fallen through. But now that it was a done deal, she couldn't be happier for him. And them, with her own job as a DHS special agent still intact.

"I thought so." He sipped more wine and then gave her a big smile. "There's more…"

"More…?" She listened intently.

"It just so happens that I am very much in love with you," Russell said earnestly. "But the only way that love can be complete for me is if it's in the context of husband and wife. So, with that being said…" He paused long enough to remove a small velvet box from the inside pocket of his solid weave blazer. Opening it to reveal a ring, he continued, "I wonder if you would do me the great honor, Rosamund Santiago, and make me the happiest man in the world, by marrying me and, if you like, raising a family together?"

Russell took the ring out and Rosamund put a hand to her mouth with sheer exhilaration. Before he could change his mind, she grabbed the fourteen-karat, two-tone gold, pear-shaped halo frame diamond engagement ring and slid it onto her finger. It was a perfect fit.

"Can I take that as a yes?" he asked lightheartedly.

"Yes, yes, and yes!" she declared enthusiastically, marveling at the ring before meeting his eyes. "I will gladly marry you, Russell Lynley. Nothing would make me happier than to become your wife. And also, the mother of our children." Whether two, three, or even four kids, they could decide that in time.

"Those words are music to my ears." Russell beamed, and scooted over in the booth to give her a hearty kiss. "Thank you."

"The pleasure is all mine." Rosamund giggled. She kissed him again, feeling giddy, and admired the ring. "We should probably have a big wedding, so we can invite all of your family, my family, and even some of our friends and coworkers we left behind in Weconta Falls." She especially wanted to invite Tracy Sheridan, whom she had stayed in contact with, and Shailene McEnany, who had provided Rosamund with a job to keep busy while living a life as Tisha González.

"I wouldn't have it any other way," Russell said in complete agreement.

Rosamund laughed. "Somehow, I didn't think you would."

"Shall we seal the deal again with another kiss?"

"Do you even need to ask?" she said, before doing the honors.

Epilogue

Homeland Security Investigations Special Agent Rosamund Santiago was in on a major crackdown on human trafficking in Texas. Following the convictions and life sentences of Simon Griswold and Harold Paxton, she had been reassigned to the HSI Houston Field Office six months ago. There, Rosamund cherished her role in taking down those individuals who would seek to sexually exploit women and children or coerce those trafficked into domestic servitude with no moral compass. Working as part of the Human Trafficking Rescue Alliance of the U.S. Southern District of Texas that brought together law enforcement agencies on the federal, state, and local levels, the Department of Homeland Security was more than happy to play its part in successful operations. Such as the latest case involving the rescue of more than two dozen undocumented minors who were being sex trafficked across Houston and otherwise kept as prisoners at a house on the north-west side of the city. The six adult traffickers were placed under arrest and would be fully prosecuted.

Beyond work and a new location to call home, Rosamund could barely believe how much her life had changed for the better, now that Russell Lynley had entered it. With a huge wedding planned for midyear, he had proven to be everything she could have ever asked for in a fiancé and future husband. That included actually working in the same city and occasionally even together in crossover investigations. On the personal front, they both wanted children and had even taken to picking out potential names for them, depending on whether male or female. And they had pooled their resources and purchased a big two-story house on Moody Street with all the trimmings and a large backyard, in anticipation of starting a family and giving them something to grow into. Not to mention, a place spacious enough to accommodate the numerous visits from their families and friends that were expected.

Having completed her work shift, Rosamund headed home just long enough to change into running attire for a date with Russell at their favorite spot for jogging and enjoying quality time together. As he never seemed to be late, she stepped up the pace, before hopping in her crimson red Subaru Forester Sport and heading off to the park.

RUSSELL CONSIDERED IT a stroke of luck and more that he was able to secure a spot with the Bureau,

based at its FBI Houston Field Office. As an experienced special agent, he was given choice assignments, along with the full confidence of the special
agent in charge, Jacquelyn Hernandez. But more im-
portantly, he got to do his thing in Houston, where
his gorgeous fiancée, Rosamund Santiago, was em-
ployed as an HSI special agent. After her ordeal in
Dallas, including losing her partner, Johnnie Langford, and being forced into the WITSEC, Russell had
expected that she might put in for a transfer to some-
place where she could start fresh. It was something
he had needed as well, having tried to escape his
troubles in St. Louis after the tragic death of his wife
and daughter by fleeing to Northern California. As
it turned out, he discovered that he didn't belong in
Weconta Falls after all, at least not for the long run.

But that move had allowed him to meet the waitress Tisha González, who had more layers beneath
the attractive surface than he was able to peel back.
He and Rosamund clicked and fell in love, giving
Russell every reason in the world to want to face
his own demons and jumpstart his career with the
Bureau. So far, it had proven to be a perfect fit. He
had just wrapped up a domestic terrorism case in
southeast Texas and, as part of an FBI Violent Crime
Task Force, moved on to an investigation of an armed
bank robbery on the northeast side of Houston.

After work, Russell changed into his jogging
clothes and climbed in his Jeep Grand Wagoneer for

a workout date with Rosamund at Hackberry Park on South Dairy Ashford Road. He was running late, but suspected he would still beat her there. Both passionate about staying in shape and jogging, in particular, it was a great bonding experience, now that they were more settled in their careers and location. He loved their new house and was happy they were both able to sell their separate residences. The new house was in a great neighborhood and was a perfect place to raise a family. He couldn't wait till they were married and could get started in that respect, as he felt they were certain to be wonderful parents. Just as Russell felt his own parents were and Rosamund's continued to be from what he could see. He looked forward to their families bonding over time and having visits back and forth. Rosamund had even talked about getting a dog when time permitted, and had told him about the Jack Russell terrier she had as a little girl.

When he arrived at the park, Russell was still hopeful he could get in a quick warm-up before Rosamund arrived. Only she had beaten him there and was already in her element as a runner, waiting for him on the jogging trail. "Finally decided to show up, huh?" she teased him.

"Sorry I'm late," he said. "Traffic and all that."

"Yeah, right. Any excuse to try to justify your tardiness, Special Agent Lynley."

Russell grinned, knowing when he had come up

short. "Guilty as charged," he relented. "Come on, let's run."

Rosamund smiled. "I'll try my best not to leave you behind."

He laughed. "Sounds like a challenge to me."

"Maybe it is."

"You're on," he accepted.

She took off down the scenic trail, leaving him in the dust, before Russell caught up and ran parallel with her. "So, how was your day?" he asked. Rosamund brought him up-to-date and asked the same. He beamed. "Honestly, it got a whole lot better the moment I laid eyes on my stunning fiancée."

She blushed. "Oh, that's what every woman wants to hear, whether true or not."

"It's true," Russell promised, taking her hand and slowing them down. "I love you, Rosamund, and you'll always be the very best part of my day."

"You know what," she uttered, "I feel exactly the same way, Russell. Maybe it's something in the water here."

He laughed. "More likely, it's something in the heart and soul."

Rosamund's face lit up. "I like that answer much better." She wrapped her arms around his neck and kissed him on the lips. "So much better."

Russell felt his heart skip a beat, before he stopped the kiss long enough to say, "Me too."

* * * * *

The Lynleys of Law Enforcement miniseries from R. Barri Flowers continues next month with Christmas Lights Killer.

Look for it wherever Harlequin Intrigue books are sold!

#2175 DEAD MAN'S HAND
A Colt Brothers Investigation • by B.J. Daniels

Despite their criminal families, DJ Diamond and Sadie Montclair dream of going legit. Until a deadly poker game—one last con—forces them to hide out together in a snowbound cabin. But will the killers, the dangerous weather or their own burgeoning attraction be their ultimate downfall?

#2176 TROUBLE IN TEXAS
The Cowboys of Cider Creek • by Barb Han

Investigating the past might cost Reese Hayes her life. Single dad rancher Darren Pierce won't turn his back on his former flame...not when her life depends on his help. But then their dangerous reunion places Darren—and his toddler twins—in the crosshairs.

#2177 KILLER ON KESTREL TRAIL
Eagle Mountain: Critical Response • by Cindi Myers

SAR volunteer Tony Meissner found his friend's murdered body twenty years ago. Now the deceased's younger sister, Kelsey Chapman, is in town, searching for answers. But will their joint investigation expose a cold-case killer determined to stay hidden...or place them next on the kill list?

#2178 THE SECRET SHE KEEPS
A Tennessee Cold Case Story • by Lena Diaz

Time is running out for lawyer Raine Quintero's brother, who is wrongly on death row. Making a bargain with Callum Wright is her sole hope. If only she wasn't so attracted to the charismatic private investigator...or keeping dangerous secrets to ensure his cooperation on the case.

#2179 CLOSING IN ON CLUES
Beaumont Brothers Justice • by Julie Anne Lindsey

Nicole Homes knows her sister's disappearance is no accident. The police won't help—but her former love PI Dean Beaumont will. He's familiar with Nicole's difficult upbringing and the pitfalls she and her sister faced. But resurrecting the past—and the attraction that comes with it—could be a deadly game.

#2180 CHRISTMAS LIGHTS KILLER
The Lynleys of Law Enforcement • by R. Barri Flowers

Silent night, deadly night? Sheriff's detective Annette Lynley is determined to catch the Christmas Lights Killer. Then Hamilton McCade's missing niece turns up dead. Partnering with the capable state trooper is a complication her investigation doesn't need. Neither is falling for him in the face of danger...

HARLEQUIN
PLUS

Try the best multimedia subscription service for romance readers like you!

Read, Watch and Play.

Experience the easiest way to get the romance content you crave.

Start your **FREE TRIAL** at
<u>www.harlequinplus.com/freetrial</u>.